DREW LECLAIR
CRUSHES THE CASE

DREW LECLAIR
CRUSHES THE CASE

BY KATRYN BURY

CLARION BOOKS

An Imprint of HarperCollins*Publishers*

Clarion Books is an imprint of HarperCollins Publishers.

Drew Leclair Crushes the Case

www.harpercollinschildrens.com

ISBN 978-0-35-870152-1

23 24 25 26 27 LBC 5 4 3 2 1

First Edition

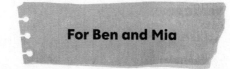

For Ben and Mia

1

TWENTY-TWO GRAPES. THAT'S HOW MANY it took for our school librarian, Mr. Covacha, to notice that something was afoot.

My best friend, Shrey, always rolls his eyes when I use words like *afoot*. "Drew," he says, "why are you always talking like those old British detectives?"

Okay, so he's not wrong.

But I knew something was up by the third grape. Three is kind of a magical number in criminal profiling. My hero, Dr. Lita Miyamoto, says that after three crimes you know a perpetrator doesn't just have a motive, they have an *obsession*.

Ever since the book fair preview last week, Mr. Covacha had been finding grapes around the fair. The weird thing? They were *single* grapes. One on the shelves, one by the register, and one balanced atop the pyramid-style book displays. When I volunteered to help around the fair, I started to find them too. Each grape was so far spread out that it was clear these kids weren't randomly dropping snacks.

This was *deliberate*.

It was all I could do not to track down the perpetrators myself. I kept reminding myself that I was under strict orders: no more snooping. Even when I'm *not* trying, though, the answers often find me.

First, I noticed that the grapes appeared only after sixth grade lunch. Yesterday, I'd casually noted to Mr. Covacha that I'd seen Dante King and Sukhjot Kaur at the book fair every day. But the final clue was too much for me to disregard. Today, I saw Dante and Sukhjot passing each other grapes when *mandarin oranges* were on the school lunch menu. I mean, you can't ignore that, right?

Still, it was hard to hand over the names to Mr. Covacha without explaining to him about the modus operandi. Not to mention the fact that the perpetrators were so clearly escalating. But school mysteries are something I promised to leave behind. Especially since, so far, they've only gotten me:

1) An in-school suspension

2) Ostracized by my peers

3) Forced to talk about my feelings every night with my dad, who I'd way rather be watching true crime documentaries with.

So, I'm doing the regular-kid thing. Which is why I'm watching Mr. Covacha perform the laziest interrogation I've ever seen in my years of watching detective shows.

"Hey, kiddos," he says, leaning over a nervous-looking Dante and Sukhjot. They're caught and they know it. "I know this is going to sound . . . well, a little silly. But, have you two been leaving grapes around the book fair this week?"

Squeezing my eyes shut, I imagined how it would be if I were asking the questions. In my mind, I would be like a British detective, declaring my deductive process as the suspects squirmed.

"A. Single. Grape," I would say emphatically, slowly pacing the displays. "In point of fact, *twenty-two* single grapes. To be fair, grapes *were* on the lunch menu that first day. But why, then, would the grapes be so deliberately placed? One grape on the graphic novels. One on the historical fiction display. One balanced between two *Fortnite* books." Then I would swing around, eyes wide, pointing at Dante. "*You* like *Fortnite*, don't you, Dante?"

A smile instinctively tugs at the corners of my mouth

as I imagine myself with a Sherlock Holmes–esque cap, talking the perpetrators into a corner. But then, a real confession jerks me out of the fantasy.

"Okay!" Sukhjot says, looking up at Mr. Covacha with a frown. "We thought it would be funny!"

"We didn't think anyone would notice!" Dante jumps in. "It's not like we took anything, or ruined any books. I mean, kids are stealing erasers all the time! And I know one kid took the big World Records book! I'm pretty sure I saw him do it."

My ears perk up at this. I'd noticed that book missing a few days ago, and I knew that Mr. Covacha already suspected someone. I swear, I don't *mean* to overhear conversations. Sometimes it just happens.

From behind the counter, I stare at Mr. Covacha, willing him to ask a follow-up question.

"I see," Mr. Covacha says, rubbing his chin as if he's trying to figure out what to ask next. "Well . . ."

I feel as if my head might explode.

Ask him who did it! He knows! Just ASK!

Fortunately, Dante is more than willing to blab without Mr. Covacha's help.

"It was a big kid," Dante tells him. "He's white, with blond hair and a really pink face. Like he's embarrassed or blushing or something—but all the time."

I mentally keep track of the details. *White, pinkish complexion, tall or heavyset . . .* That totally fits with Aiden Rullhausen—the kid I'd overheard Mr. Covacha talking about with Vice Principal Lopez.

"Okay, Alan. Thanks for telling me that," Mr. Covacha says.

"We're sorry, Mr. Covacha," Sukhjot and Dante say in unison.

Then, after this complete nothing-burger of an interrogation, Mr. Covacha says, "Thanks, kiddos. You can go back to class. Just cut it out with the grapes, okay?" He walks behind the desk next to me and dismisses the two sixth graders with a wave.

When they've shuffled out, I turn to Mr. Covacha. I'm sure that my usually pale and freckled complexion is crimson due to the whole head-nearly-exploding from a few minutes earlier. So, I try to sound as casual as possible when I say, "Well, I guess it was that Aiden Rullhausen kid you thought it was. Who stole the Guinness World Records book, I mean."

Mr. Covacha gives me an appraising look over the tip of his glasses. "How did you know I thought it was Aiden?"

My face heats up, and I imagine I must be full tomato color by now. "You talk pretty loud."

"You're very observant, aren't you, Drew?"

"Some say that," I tell him with a shrug. "Usually while they're yelling at me."

He laughs. "I like observant. It makes for a good librarian, you know. Think about it."

I've got another career path in mind, but I still beam up at him. "Thanks, Mr. Covacha."

He looks at his office. "All right, I'll give Vice Principal Lopez a call about that stolen book now. Will you be okay running the counter?"

I give him a thumbs-up and watch as he slips into his office and closes the door. I'd agreed to stay to help during lunch today, but the rush usually doesn't start for another ten minutes, until after kids eat their food. I reach into my backpack and pull out my notebook, opening it to a page I'd marked: *Book Fair Grape Prank*.

Even though I'm not *technically* solving mysteries right now, I like to keep good records. That can't get me in trouble, right?

"Drew!" A voice cuts through my haze.

"What?!" I say a bit defensively, jumping out of my chair as if caught. I relax when I see that it's Shrey and Trissa.

My two best friends exchange an identical worried expression. Other than that, they look about as different as can be. Since Shrey grew another few inches this year, he towers above a petite Trissa. Also, while Shrey usually opts for a sports jersey and jeans, Trissa likes to wear the brightest colors under the sun. Even her new glasses are a brilliant violet color, with a faux jewel trim.

"Sorry, I'm just jumpy today," I explain my reaction. Shoving my hand into the mess that is my backpack, I retrieve my pen. Then, I cast a sidelong look at them, hoping they won't bring up the Big Thing that's happening this weekend.

I'm *so* not ready to talk about that.

Fortunately, Shrey doesn't push. "Your skull game is next level right now," he says appreciatively, looking down at the doodles in my notebook.

I beam at him, glancing at my latest skull. I've been drawing them since I was in preschool, which freaked out every adult in the vicinity (other than my dad). But at least I have friends who don't mind my preoccupation with the macabre.

"It's this new ink," I tell them. "My dad got it for me online. It's called Alchemist's Dungeon."

"That is so you." Shrey laughs.

"Right?!" Lovingly, I brush my fingers over my black-and-silver fountain pen, inscribed with the words *It will be me*. "I still can't believe Lita gave this to me," I murmur.

A few months earlier, I'd gotten to meet Dr. Miyamoto, which was pretty much the high point of my entire life. When my dad had embarrassingly gushed to her about my dream to become a criminal profiler, she'd given me a pen.

Okay, okay, I know. A pen isn't exactly exciting. And it's not like it was her personal note-taking pen or anything. From what she told Dad while I was blubbering, it sounded like a fan group had made her an engraved set.

Still, it felt like she was passing a torch to me. Like when Thor gets his hammer, or a Jedi gets their lightsaber. It felt weighty, like it *meant* something.

That's the other reason I'd been trying to lay off the school mysteries. A *big* reason, actually. Lita had given me a pen, but she also told me I should really pursue profiling as a career. You know what future well-renowned profilers *don't* usually do? Get suspended from school for breaking into the school office to get evidence. I imagine that's not the kind of record the FBI is looking for when they hire.

"You're so in love with that pen," Trissa says with a laugh. "I think I hear wedding bells . . ." She cups her hand to her ear playfully.

"Ha-ha." I shove her playfully over the counter. "Lita

told me that every profiler should have a good one, that's all. Hey, are you guys sticking around for the full lunch period, by the way? I thought you were eating with Connor."

"We were going to," Shrey says, "but we ate fast. And he's off rehearsing with Brian Wu, since they just found out they got Kristoff and Hans in the *Frozen* musical. We just thought we'd see—" He breaks off, his eyes wide.

OBSERVATIONS:

- Shrey is suddenly and very visibly sweating.
- His eyes keep darting back to the door.
- His dark brown skin is flushing an even deeper shade.

CONCLUSION: Shrey's latest mega-crush, Zora Scurlock, must be around here somewhere.

"Pretend we're talking," he demands in a stage whisper.

"We *are* talking," Trissa states.

"No, like, pretend we're *deep* in conversation."

I follow his gaze and see two girls walk past the counter, book fair passes in hand. Yep, it's Zora Scurlock—and her best friend, Alix Chang. I turn back to face Shrey with a smirk.

"So this *is* a Zora Scurlock thing," I say, crossing my arms.

Ever since the beginning of December, Shrey has been mooning over her. Apparently, she started saying *"hola"* to him in Spanish class. Which is all Shrey needs to fall *madly in love*.

"Not that it's a problem," Trissa says. "I'm on the Shrey and Zora train. She's in the Random Acts of Kindness club with me and she's *really* nice. Also, frankly, we could use some more Black girl magic in our detective group."

"Agree, I can't help on that front," I say, waving a hand around my super-white face.

"You are really holding up that end," Shrey adds.

"I am. Thank you," Trissa says with a nod. "Anyway, I like her. And Alix seems chill, too. This could be a thing!"

"Are you more interested in Zora for *me* or for our friend group?" Shrey asks.

Trissa grins. "Can't it be both? It's been kind of a bummer since Holly moved to Berkeley and Connor is so busy all the time with theater, and with helping out at his mom's restaurant after school. Look, all I'm saying is I'm one hundred percent pro-Zorey," she says, then grimaces. "Shr . . . ora? No, that's awful. Scur-hotra?"

"Please stop," Shrey pleads.

"Trissa, you ship *everyone*," I point out. "I didn't even know the *word* 'ship' until you came into our lives. You shipped Principal El-Sayed and the UPS guy last week."

"Okay, first of all, there was a *vibe* when that UPS guy came into the office," Trissa says. "Second of all, Zora is our *people*. She and Shrey—"

"SHHH!" Shrey shushes us far louder than we're speaking and both Zora and Alix turn to stare at us.

"Don't stereotype us librarians, Shrey, GOD!" I shout, pretending he'd made a joke.

Trissa laughs loudly, and the two girls turn back toward the fair.

"Thanks for the cover," Shrey mutters, looking between us.

Trissa leans back in and lowers her voice. "If you like her so much, why don't you talk to her, instead of pretending to have conversations we're already having."

"I'm working on it, okay?" Shrey says. "I said one word to her last week. No wait, three! '*Me llamo Shrey.*' We were in the same group for our conversation unit in Spanish."

I regard him with a dry expression. "Wow. Three whole words last week. Slow down there, Flash."

I'm teasing him but, deep down, I'm actually relieved that he likes someone else. After Shrey tried to kiss me back in October, there were weeks of weirdness that felt like years. After we made friends with Trissa, it got better. But it took a long time for us to feel normal again.

"Whatever, I'm bold," he retorts weakly. "I'm *Oakland* strong."

"Sure you are, buddy." Trissa pats Shrey's shoulder sympathetically.

I bite my lip to avoid saying that he's really not meeting the threshold of our city's "Oakland strong" motto while cowardly hiding from a crush. Trissa says that sometimes I can be *too* blunt. What would be the right thing to say here? Something about being yourself?

I'm about to wing it when I see Zora break off from Alix and head toward the library counter. Shrey's face immediately goes slack again, but he manages not to make any weird noises, at least.

"Hi, Zora!" I say brightly. "What can I do for you?"

"I've got two holds ready," she says. She smiles at Trissa. "Hey, Trissa."

Trissa gives the world's most obvious look and says "Heyyy, Zora," in a singsong voice. I can practically hear

Shrey's blood pressure rising.

I turn to the holds and look through the *S* section until I find a young-adult fantasy novel and a nonfiction book on Bay Area earthquakes labeled: SCURLOCK, Z.

"Getting ready for the next big one?" I ask Zora, scanning the nonfiction book and handing it to her. "Or is this for school?"

"Personal research," Zora says, looking embarrassed as she glances at Shrey.

Huh. Maybe there's more than a chance that she knows he exists.

When I grab the second book to scan it, a small folded piece of paper falls out. I'm momentarily startled, but manage to grab the paper before it ends up on the ground. Maybe the last borrower was using it as a bookmark? I move to unfold the paper and put it in our Lost and Found cubby when Zora cries out, "Um, that's mine!"

I glance down at the paper but she reaches for it before I can read all of it. I catch the words *have* and *bracelet* but that's it.

"Sorry," Zora apologizes. "Um, I didn't finish it last time and that was my bookmark."

I narrow my eyes. Really? Something about her

explanation doesn't add up.

Still, I don't want to ruin Shrey's chances with Zora by interrogating her. And I shouldn't be looking for mysterious things anymore, right?

"No problem," I say, tucking the paper back into the book.

Zora is visibly relieved. "Thanks, Drew. Um, see you in Spanish, Shrey."

After a noticeable, tongue-tied delay, Shrey manages to repeat, "See you in Spanish." Zora waves and heads back to find Alix.

"Did you hear that?" Shrey whispers as soon as they're out of earshot. "Four words!"

"Yeah," I mumble distractedly, still staring after Zora.

"Wait. I know that face," Shrey says, narrowing his eyes at me. "What is it? Did I say 'See you in Spanish' wrong? I did, didn't I?" Shrey begins to spiral. "Wait, did I say 'see,' the word, or 'C,' the letter? Can you even tell the difference? 'See,' 'C,' 'see,' 'C,' 's—'"

Rolling my eyes, I interrupt his diatribe. "No," I say in a hushed tone. "It was that note. It looked like the letters were made from cut-out newsprint and magazines."

"Meaning . . . ?" Shrey asks.

I swallow. "It looked like a *ransom note*."

2

AS USUAL, MY BEST FRIENDS have totally opposite reactions.

Trissa's dark brown eyes shine as she says, "Oooh. A *ransom* note?"

Shrey, our group skeptic, immediately scoffs. "Come on. A ransom note? Do those even exist in real life?"

I give him a Look. "You must know I'm about to tell you every instance of ransom notes in true crime history. Lita Miyamoto says—"

"All right, all right," Shrey cuts me off. "You know more than I do on this subject. Why do you think it's a ransom note?"

"The cut-out style letters are usually an attempt to hide someone's handwriting. Why would someone hide their handwriting unless they're doing something bad?"

Trissa's eyes flit back and forth. My other best friend is definitely our ace at human relations, and I can tell she's trying to find a way to say something diplomatically.

"I get that," Trissa says. "But it could be private notes between Zora and Alix."

I gaze down at my notebook.

THE PLAN:

1) Get a 4.0 GPA from now through high school (and NO MORE suspensions).
2) Get into a college with a good sociology and criminology program.
3) Join the FBI and become the next world-renowned profiler.

"Yeah, you're probably right," I say, closing my book with a sigh.

"Hey," Trissa says softly, looking at me worriedly for a second time. "That doesn't sound like you, to give up on a theory."

"Maybe this is about . . . uhhh, never mind." Shrey glances at Trissa, who gives him a warning look.

Hastily I busy myself by grabbing a duster and

16

sweeping it across my keyboard. I can see the handwriting on the wall. They are *definitely* about to bring up the topic I've been avoiding for a week now.

"Are you sure you're not looking for anything to distract you from your mom coming this weekend?" Shrey blurts, cringing as though I might kick him.

For a second, I think I might.

"It's possible," I say through gritted teeth.

Truth be told, I've been volunteering for everything I can at school. Also, I've been doing extra chores and getting ahead on my homework. That last one is technically part of the Plan, but it's possible I'd do *anything* to make me forget that this is Mom's first visit since she left us.

That's right, I haven't seen my mom in *three months*. She didn't even come back for Christmas, since she and her new boyfriend, Dustin (a.k.a. my old guidance counselor, Mr. Clark), were busy moving into a condo in Hanalei Bay. At first, they were living in a luxury yurt, but that didn't last long. My mom isn't exactly known for sticking with things. Like parenting.

"When's she flying in, anyway?" Trissa asks, breaking me out of what was rapidly becoming a rage spiral.

"Saturday afternoon," I mutter. "Three twenty."

"Is she staying . . . like, with you guys, or . . . ?" Shrey trails off. "Sorry. I don't know how this separation thing works."

"She's not staying with us. She got a room at the Clearview, up in the hills."

"Fancy!" Trissa says. "I'll bet you can at least get some spa time, or some good food out of it. I wonder if they have those tater tots with basil. Fancy tater tots are totally a thing." Trissa licks her lips.

"Tater tots are okay," I concede. I can tell she's trying to be positive but I'm not feeling ready to be positive about anything concerning Mom. At least I still have a few days to prepare.

"Hey," Shrey says. "If you want to talk about it . . ."

Brrrriiinnnng!

"Oops, saved by the bell!" I say, looking fake-disappointed. Grabbing my bag, I move past them to leave.

"You have to talk about it eventually," Shrey calls after me.

"Shrey, take a hint. She doesn't want to talk about it now!" I glance back and smile as I see Trissa, clearly scolding him.

As I walk out of the library, I can feel my shoulders hunch over. I may want to kick Shrey a large portion of the time, but he is right. I have been finding ways to distract myself since I found out that Mom is coming.

Every time I think about her in our house, I think of the last time I saw her there. She was standing in the doorway with her bags packed, completely ready to leave us with no warning. I can actually see it in my mind— her phony tears, and even the burgundy sweater she was wearing that Dad always liked. When the memory comes to me, it hits me as if it just happened yesterday, and it hits hard. Like one of those anvils in old cartoons.

Splat.

Mom had written me a letter "explaining" the move and how much she still loves me, but how can she? How does a mother who loves her kid decide to move 2,457 miles away?

Yes, I mapped it. Of *course* I mapped it. After she left in October, I knew my parents were probably not going to live together. But I never thought she would move there. She *literally* moved away from me.

The thought, as usual, makes my chest tighten and my breathing start to shallow. As I climb the steps toward my technology class, I hear a faint wheeze at the back of my throat. Reaching down, I grab the rescue inhaler from my pocket and take a deep puff.

Maybe I should talk to Dad about all this. Or take my friends up on their offer and get it off my chest.

But I was afraid that, the more I thought about it, the more anxious I would be. And the more anxious I get, the more I tend to make what Dad calls "little errors in judgment."

Nope. Not today, stress monster.

Instead, I try to actually pay attention in technology class. By the time I get to my Core class (language arts and history—the last two periods of the day), I'm fried. If I can't stop myself from stressing, maybe I can calm myself down another way. Surreptitiously, I slip one of my Bluetooth earbuds in, pressing play on the phone I have obscured in my bag.

Lately, I've become obsessed with this new podcast called *Game Over* by these true crime podcasters named Gerald Burgess and Max Echeverria. It's based on the hunt for a notorious art thief, the Masterpiece Man. Lita Miyamoto tracked him down (because of course she did) after five years of high-end art thefts. He would leave notes behind that simply said "GAME OVER" with his signature in the corner, like a painting. Hence the name.

In today's episode, we will cover the infamous Hale Museum theft in Annapolis. The FBI has been called in, but the Masterpiece Man is still using his calling card. Is he too smart for them?

No, I think. Not for Lita.

For a second, the notes call to mind the creepy ransom-style note I saw in Zora's library hold, but I push the thought to the side and turn the volume up. Just listening to the opening bars of the podcast theme already soothes me. That is, until an unwanted voice jars me to attention like nails on a chalkboard.

"Is that for *school?*" the voice asks pointedly.

Taking out my earbud, I whip around to glare at Emma Cruz.

She and Brie Collins are both smirking at me. Emma and Brie bullied me all through grade school. As you can imagine, they are *not* my favorite people. Unfortunately, they're also in my last two classes of the day. They've (mostly) stayed off my back since I caught Ella Baker Shade, a.k.a. Ethan Navarez. Since their best friend-slash-leader, Alicia Alongie, was one of Ethan's targets, all three of them have been flying under the radar. Maybe they're getting back to their old habits.

"Are *you* working on something for school?" I whisper pointedly, gesturing at the cell phones both of them have hidden on their laps.

Emma reddens. "Whatever, *Drew*. Get back to your snooping. It's what you're good at, right?"

Brie giggles and the two of them finally turn their

attention away from me.

Just as I'm breathing a sigh of relief, my Core teacher barks, "Copernicus! Galileo! Newton! What do they all have in common?" Ms. Woodrich stalks across the front of the room like a panther, eyeing us.

I raise my hand. "They are all major contributors to the Scientific Revolution?"

"Excellent, Drew!" Ms. Woodrich points to her smart board, where she starts going through a list of inventions starting in the mid-1500s.

Despite my best efforts, my attention starts to wander. I can't help but notice Zora and Alix sitting together a few rows away. Not that I'm thinking about Zora, or the maybe-ransom notes. I'm definitely *not*.

OBSERVATIONS:

- Alix is using her pen to make a temporary tattoo on her right hand. It looks like the water tribe symbol from *Avatar*. Very cool.
- Zora is sneaking a book into her Core textbook. The cover has a cartoon bubble that reads *Sedimentary, Dear Watson!*
- Alix finishes her tattoo and then

scrawls something on a small piece of paper and hands it secretly to Zora, who smiles.

CONCLUSIONS: Alix is a pop-culture nerd, Zora is a geology nerd, and Trissa is probably right about them passing notes.

So . . . the so-called ransom note isn't a thing. Which is good news for me.

Isn't it?

"A heliocentric universe!" Ms. Woodrich is practically shouting. "It sounds like old news to us, but to the people living in 1543, it was unheard of."

"Pssssttt."

Swiveling my head around, I see three girls whispering—Olivia Campos, Kenzie Perl, and Sarina Masoumi. I remember from my notes that they've gotten in trouble at least fifteen times for talking in class this year. Ms. Woodrich should really—

My thoughts are interrupted when Zora whispers again, this time looking right at me. "PSSSSSSST!"

I do a double take as if to say, *Me?*

Her eyes dart toward Ms. Woodrich, and then she scribbles something down in her spiral-bound notebook.

After a moment, she rips the page out, folds it up, and kicks it to me.

What the *what*?

Is this going to be a girl thing? Is she about to ask me if Shrey likes her or something? Ugh. Why does it seem like every kid in the universe is pairing up into couples? I find the idea nauseating, for the following reasons:

1) Kissing is objectively gross. Why not just blow your nose on someone? Equally germy.

2) Holding hands = same problem. Viruses, people!

3) The term *crush* makes it sound like a horrible accident. Like you got flattened by an elephant.

My heart rate ratchets back up as I open the folded paper. When I read it, I look up at Zora with surprise, and then back down at the note:

> Shrey told me what you said about the note in
> my library book. You were right. Someone is out to
> get me and I need your help!

3

AN HOUR AND A FEW low-key texts later, I meet
Shrey and Trissa to fill them in before Zora meets us
after school.

There are a few secret spots I have around campus—
places where I can hide from the crowds but also
observe. The dirt-lined path behind the STEM building
isn't good for people-watching, but it keeps us out of
sight. Most of the students don't know it exists—sort of
like a hidden passageway to a secret garden. If that secret
garden mostly consisted of a chain-link fence, dirt, and
the occasional piece of trash. Okay, it's not picturesque.
But it *is* the best for covert meetings.

Of course, Shrey is currently making things . . . less
than covert.

"Zora Scurlock is meeting us. Zora. SCURLOCK!"
he sputters.

"You've said that, like, a dozen times," I point out. "Do you know other words?"

"But . . . *Zora Scurlock* is *meeting* us." His eyes are wild and sweat trickles down his forehead. "I mean, I told her to talk to you. I know that. But I didn't think . . . Do I look okay?"

Trissa and I exchange a smirk

"Oh my God. That's a no," he moans.

Trissa unzips her EBMS hoodie, revealing a vibrant, mint-colored Baby Yoda shirt underneath. "Here. Wipe off your face," she instructs, handing him the sweatshirt.

Trissa isn't a rule-breaker, but she does like to push the envelope by wearing outfits under her uniform that aren't exactly dress-code friendly. Bright colors, flip sequins, and character tees are in her daily rotation. It's a whole commitment-to-fashion thing.

"I don't know why you're freaking out anyway," she goes on. "Zora's not a celebrity. She's a nerd, like us."

"Wait, really?" Shrey asks. "But she's so pretty."

Trissa does a double take. "Um, excuse me?"

I glare at him. "Yeah, *excuse* me?"

"No, I mean! Um, not like you and Drew aren't pretty. It's, um—"

Fortunately for Shrey, this is the moment Zora and Alix round the corner.

"Um, hi," Zora says shyly, looking between us. "You all know Alix?"

We nod, and Alix gives us a salute.

Shrey says, "Hi, Zora," in a weirdly deep voice.

Zora looks at Shrey and then clasps her hands together. "Okay, then, I guess I'll get right to it. I heard about how you caught Ella Baker Shade, and I asked Shrey if this is a regular thing with you."

"It is *totally* a regular thing," Shrey speaks for me. "She's all about the mysteries."

Zora doesn't seem to notice my immediate glaring at Shrey, and goes on. "I'm hoping you can help me with this. Something was stolen from me—a bracelet. It's a Xavier and Xo charm bracelet." She holds up a selfie with Alix on her phone that shows the silver charm bracelet. I spot a heart charm with engraving, and a deep red moon-shaped stone. I can't help but notice that Alix has a similar bracelet on, both today and in the photo.

"We got them at the same time," Alix explains, seeing my expression.

"That makes sense," I say. "Xavier and Xo. Is that an expensive brand?" I instinctively look to Trissa for confirmation.

Trissa nods. "But the charms don't all look like Xavier

27

and Xo. Do you get them from somewhere else?"

Zora's glance flit over to Alix as she says, "Some are original, and some I like to make. Anyway, I always take off all of my jewelry during PE and keep it in the lockers."

"Wait," Trissa says, looking surprised. "It was stolen from your *PE* locker? Like, the ones next to the changing rooms?"

Zora blinks. "Yeah, why?"

Trissa directs her attention to me. "Remember I told you the other day that my friend Liz thought someone stole her Harper Berry eye shadow palette?"

"Whoa," Alix says. "Harper Berry. Very chichi."

"I know," Trissa says. "Her parents saved up to get it for her birthday. It was a really big deal to lose it."

Alix nudges Zora. "That tracks with the Preethi thing!"

"Oh, yeah," Zora says. "Like two weeks ago, I over-heard Preethi Agarwal talking. She was really upset, talking about how someone had taken her cell phone out of her locker. Then, another girl—I think her name is Jasmine—came up and said something like 'Not again!'"

Shrey, Trissa, and I exchange looks.

"Things go missing a lot on a school campus. But

28

it is odd that they all seem to be centered in the PE area—" I break off, remembering something. "You know, I actually overheard a boy talking about his watch going missing a week or two ago. Juan Madrigal. He's in my science class. Maybe that was stolen from the lockers too."

"I'm surprised you didn't mention it," Shrey says.

I bite my lip. Of *course* I'd been curious about Juan's missing watch. Especially after Trissa had mentioned her friend Liz missing her makeup. It was one of the many things I'd tried to ignore since I resolved to never get in trouble again. Also, like I said, things go missing at this school a lot. But for them to have been taken from the same place . . .

"I wonder if the others got the notes," Zora mumbles, breaking me out of my thoughts.

"You said I was right about the *note* today," I point out. "But you just said 'notes.' Were there more?"

Zora sighs. "Yeah. That's where it gets *weird*. Today was actually the second note. Last Wednesday I came back and everything was in my locker except my bracelet. Like, they left my phone, my wallet, and other jewelry. I wasn't even sure it was stolen. Until . . . *this*." She thrusts a piece of paper into my hand. "This is the note I got first."

I lower my eyes and read the note.

MISSING ANYTHING? STAY TUNED FOR INSTRUCTIONS.

"That's really weird," Trissa says.

Alix snorts. "Yeah. Bananas, right? It reminds me of something a creepy killer would send."

"You sound like Drew," Shrey points out.

"He's not wrong," I admit, smiling at Alix. I stop short of rambling about the Masterpiece Man, though. I've learned that people tend to back away slowly when I talk about true crime.

Zora sighs, handing me a second piece of paper. "Well, if you think that's strange, check this out."

I HAVE YOUR BRACELET. YOU CAN GET IT BACK FOR $50. WAIT FOR LOCATION. DON'T TELL ANYONE. YOU ARE BEING WATCHED.

"Whoa" is all I can manage to say. "That's . . . ominous."

"Right?!" Zora says, her eyes wide. "Anyhow, that's the note you saw today. Shrey asked me how I was doing today in Spanish and . . . it kind of spilled out. He said you could help me."

I look at Shrey a bit irritably but ask her, "Were *both* notes in your library holds?"

"Yeah."

"How often do you pick up holds?" I ask.

"Like, all the time," Alix says, grinning. "Well, at least two or three times a week."

"So, we'd be looking at someone who knows your movements well enough to know that you pick up library holds on a regular basis," Trissa says.

Zora squirms. "*Knows my movements.* Just like that note. They *are* watching me."

"I—I'm sure no one is actually watching you," Shrey fumbles. "Not that you're a person who, like, fades into the background—you're definitely not! I mean, people *notice* you. I don't know *who* notices, but, um, I . . ." He looks at us desperately as if begging us to save him from a full verbal meltdown.

"What Shrey means is that you don't seem like the kind of person who'd have enemies," Trissa rushes to cut him off. "Can we ask—how was the bracelet meaningful to you?"

"One of the charms had an inscription, that's all," Zora says slowly. "It wouldn't be special to anyone else."

I narrow my eyes.

OBSERVATIONS:

- Zora and Alix trade another look.
- Alix tugs at her own colorful charm bracelet—the one that's nearly identical to Zora's.

CONCLUSIONS: There's something about the bracelet they're not telling us.

I consider calling them on the look, but hold back. I'm not even sure if I want to take this case . . . yet.

"One more question, if that's okay," I say. "Do you regularly lock your PE locker?"

She lowers her eyes. "Sometimes I forget. I think I did that day, but I'm not sure."

"Hey, you've got one up on me," Shrey offers. "I always forget to use my lock because I never get my own combination right. Also, I figure nobody's going to want my school uniform."

Zora beams at Shrey gratefully. "Glad I'm not the only one."

Alix suddenly gives *me* a look, and I wonder if she's trying to tell me something. Does she know that Shrey likes Zora? I wish I were better at this secret girl language.

"So, do you really think you can find Zora's bracelet?" Alix asks.

My face heats up. Asking questions and getting all the information felt natural, but actually investigating a series of thefts? That sounds a lot like something that could jeopardize the Plan. That being said, the way Alix is looking at me hopefully makes me want to say yes. And Zora *is* really nice. Helping her would be the right thing to do. I look between them, feeling that imminent head-exploding sensation again.

"Can I think about it?" I ask after a long beat.

Shrey and Trissa regard me with comically dropped jaws, but Zora seems relieved that I'll even consider it.

"Of course. Thank you, *thank* you!" she gushes. "Just let me know when you decide."

She and Alix say their goodbyes and disappear around the corner of the STEM building.

When they're gone, Shrey moans in anguish, his face buried in his hands. When he looks up, he says, "Did I babble about people noticing her for, like, five minutes? And do I smell?" Shrey asks, still looking stunned. "I feel like I lost ten pounds in sweat."

Trissa leans over and takes a whiff. "I still smell deodorant," she says. "You're good."

"Really? You smell deodorant?"

"Yep. Fresh, even," Trissa confirms, elbowing him playfully. "Keep up that scent and you could ask her to the dance."

I roll my eyes. Our annual winter dance, "Wonderland," is coming up next week, which Shrey has been obsessing about for almost as long as he's realized his love for Zora.

"Okay, now that we've established that I don't stink like week-old cheese, can we get down to what the heck Drew's problem is?" Shrey asks.

"What?" I ask, offended.

"Well, it's not exactly like you to turn down a mystery," Trissa says.

I take out my notebook and point. "But . . . the Plan!"

Shrey looks at me. "Okay. But the Plan only says that you can't get in trouble again. There's nothing that says you can't help a friend out. No suspensions needed this time. It's a Shrey guarantee!"

I roll my eyes. "You're clearly trying to get me to investigate because you want Zora to be your girlfriend. But whatever."

"It's happening to other kids, though," Trissa points out. "Like Liz, who does *not* deserve that. If things are getting stolen this much, it sounds like it's one person.

Like . . . a *serial* locker thief."

My eyes pop. Trissa sure knows how to get me intrigued.

"Okay, fine!" I relent. "What do we have so far?"

Trissa rubs her chin thoughtfully. "Well, the ransom notes being put in library books definitely stands out as important," she says. "The thief could have left the notes in the locker where the bracelet was taken. It seems like they would have to know that Zora spends a lot of time in the library, at least."

"Agreed," Shrey says. "Also, the holds area is behind the counter. I'm not saying someone couldn't sneak back there, but it would be a lot easier for a library volunteer to hide the notes, right?"

"Right," I say. "Who is the most likely suspect? Someone who needs the cash?"

"Maybe . . ." Shrey says.

"Fifty dollars is a lot of money to most kids," I say, "And if the perpetrator knows Zora, they might know she could get ahold of that. Maybe the thief realized that the bracelet wasn't as pricey as they thought. They could have decided to send the ransom note to make more money."

"How do you know how much money Zora has?" Shrey asks.

"Zora lives above the highway—in Clearview Heights, where the rich kids live," I say. "I remember her talking about her neighborhood once, so it's in the notebooks. I'm not saying Zora's parents would give her the money, but any parent who lives in that neighborhood probably has fifty bucks to give their kid."

"Fair," Shrey says. "So . . . you seem interested. Does this mean you'll do it?"

"Come on, Drew!" Trissa begs. "I could actually find Liz's Harper Berry! And Shrey could . . . get a girlfriend!"

I can't help but smile. "Okay, okay—let's do it! We can start tomorrow. Trissa, you keep an eye on Zora—"

"Why can't I keep an eye on Zora?" Shrey whines.

"Because it will look like you're stalking her," I say bluntly. "Trissa is in the Kindness Club with her, so it'll feel natural. Shrey, can you meet up with me to talk to Preethi?"

"Ugh. Preethi's always giving me the stink eye," he says. "But, fine."

"I'll ask Juan about his missing watch tomorrow to see if there's a connection. Then I'll check on the library angle, since I'm there during fifth period," I say. "Tomorrow night, we can meet at my place to compare notes. Dad's out for the evening, so we'll have the house to ourselves."

Trissa looks like she might burst. "Does this mean my first official crime board?"

Laughing, I say, "Yes, your first official crime board. But I've got to tell Dad what we're up to this time."

Both of them nod, but then Shrey's attention snaps away from us like a rubber band. "Zora!" he cries.

"Yes, I know this mystery is all about Zora," I say, "but if you're just going to say her name over and over like a broken robot—"

"No," Shrey cuts me off, pointing to a red picnic table by the office. "She and Alix are still here. Can I tell her we're officially taking the case? Can I tell her, can I tell her?"

"Fine!" I moan.

"Go on, Romeo," Trissa says, waving him off while we bust up laughing.

He doesn't need any more encouragement, running off like a puppy dog toward his new crush. For some reason, seeing him walk away from us makes me feel a little pit in my stomach. Like he's leaving us forever or something.

I try to remind myself that the more he hangs out with Zora, the easier it will be for him and me to be just friends. It will be nice, being able to hang out with Shrey again on our own—playing video games and binge-watching shows without worrying if I'm sitting too close to him. I can even have a one-on-one conversation without getting nervous that my face is too available for kissing.

Brushing the weird feeling aside, I say goodbye to Trissa. Then I put my earbuds back in to listen to *Game Over,* imagining how it would feel to catch my very own Masterpiece Man.

4

BY THE TIME I GET to Dad's bakery, Leclair's Eclairs, I'm grumpy enough to eat my weight in pastries. Technically, I'm not supposed to eat food with a high fat content, since my doctor says that both butter and stress trigger my stomachaches. And I am definitely stressed.

At least I'm in Leclair's, which is my happy place. There's something about the nonstop smell of chocolate and pastry dough that makes me feel a thousand percent better. In spite of the fact that every day brings me one step closer to a Mom Visit. I swear, I can watch true crime documentaries all day, but nothing fills me with more fear than a conversation with my mother.

What is *wrong* with me?

"Can I have five croissants?" I ask Dad as soon as I find him in the back room.

"You may have one croissant."

"So, six."

"One."

"One . . . thousand?"

Dad lets out a long-suffering sigh. "Do I need to lecture you on the food pyramid again?"

I grab a croissant off of the cooling rack. "Nah, I remember the four food groups," I say. Then I count off on my fingers. "Chocolate, coffee, and croissants, right? Oh, wait, that's three."

"I'm a failure as a father," he moans.

"You're definitely not," I assure him. I take a moment to savor the croissant, closing my eyes to experience the full effect as a buttery symphony takes place on my taste buds.

Dad tosses a glance over at our cashier, Lupe. "Drew," he says. "It's an hour until closing and the store isn't busy. Can we do our talk now?"

I resist the urge to roll my eyes. Usually, I love talking to my dad. But before Mom left, we would talk about true crime, or sweet versus sour baguettes. Now, it's all about Feelings. Dad insists on having these talks every day. It's part of *his* plan to counteract the single-parent thing, and one of the many consequences of the Ella Baker Shade incident.

Maybe I shouldn't be taking on this Zora mystery . . .

"Sure, Dad," I say. If I resist, it will only mean less time for our usual true crime binge-a-thon. Tonight I want to watch this docuseries about killer clowns, called *Painted Faces*.

Dad speaks rapidly to Lupe in Spanish, asking her to watch the counter, and then ushers me into his office. "Okay, bun," he says, "let's start with your day."

I sit down in the squishy captain's chair in front of Dad's desk and twirl around with tented fingers. "School was . . . eventful."

He looks intrigued. "Go on."

"This girl wants me to find her missing bracelet," I say carefully. He looks like he's about to go into full Dad mode, so I quickly launch into my planned monologue. "Here's the thing, Dad. It's this girl who Shrey has a crush on, so I kind of *have* to help because he asked me to. But if you *really* want me to bail on this, I will. Although I will promise you that if you let me do this, there will be no breaking the rules this time. Scout's honor."

He smirks at me. "Drew, you were never in the Scouts."

I arch my eyebrow cryptically, "That you *know* of."

Dad and I stare at each other for a long beat. Finally,

he laughs and breaks our game of eye-contact chicken. "Look, as long as you don't violate any school policies, I'm fine. Moving on, how are you feeling about seeing Mom this weekend?"

Okay, here's my chance. I can tell Dad how freaked out I am about Mom coming to visit. Like, about how I start wheezing when I picture her in our house. Or how I keep obsessively making skull drawings of Mom and Mr. Clark in Kauai, parasailing. Or how—

"Drew?"

"Um . . . I'm feeling fine about it?"

"Are you sure?"

"I guess." I absently pick at a loose piece of laminate on the corner of his desk. "As long as 'Dustin' doesn't tag along at the last minute."

"Scare quotes," Dad says, folding his hands under his chin. "Really?"

"Well, it's weird that I'm supposed to call him 'Dustin' now!" I grouse. "He was my guidance counselor, like, *yesterday.*"

"That's fair," Dad says. "Mom's friend won't be joining her for this visit. But . . ."

Dad trails off, removes his glasses and cleans them.

Ruh-roh.

This is one of Dad's "This is a serious topic" moves.

Suddenly, however, he looks down at his glasses and then back up at me.

"I keep forgetting that you know all my tells," he says.

I shift in the chair uncomfortably. "I like to call them 'behavioral indicators.'"

Ever since Mom left, I feel like every day is spent preparing for more horrible news. Is he going to tell me that they're getting married or something? Maybe Mom is insisting I live half the year with them, and 'Dustin' will try to win me over with subpar pastries from some local, low-rent bakery that doesn't even make decent malasadas.

Or . . . oh dear lord. What if Mom is *pregnant*? With a baby *Dustin*? The possibilities swirl in my head, starting to press in on each other until my stomach aches with worry. It's probably for the best that I didn't have those five extra croissants.

"I feel like I should let you know that there will be some conversations about . . . ongoing divorce proceedings."

Oh. *Divorce*. That's way easier to handle than baby Dustin.

"Dad," I say carefully. "It's okay. I know you're getting divorced. I only care that you're happy, okay?"

Dad smiles at me, and suddenly I feel a thousand

percent less awkward. His smiles make me feel safe and warm, like a thousand fresh croissants. The non-stomachache-causing kind.

"I know I was struggling after your mom left," Dad says. "But I'm doing okay. In fact, I feel like I've been getting my life back these past few weeks."

Hmmm.

OBSERVATIONS:

- Dad seems fine about divorcing Mom.
- He's been smiling at his phone a lot lately. Like he's getting funny messages from someone other than me.
- He's using phrases like "getting my life back."

CONCLUSION: Every TV show I've ever watched leads me to believe Dad's in love—or at least in "like."

"All right," I say carefully. "Anything else you want to share?"

His hands go to his face, grasping the ear pieces of his glasses. But then he releases them. "Nope," he says. "Well, other than the fact that this new scone recipe Jerry told me about is fantastic." He offers me a mandarin-glazed berry scone, but I merely narrow my eyes at him.

What the *what*? He's trying to distract me. And being shifty. Oh God. Is the thing that's making him happy *not* love, but something weird?

Did he join a cult? No. of course not. We've seen enough documentaries on modern cults. He would never fall for it. Karrie and Grace, the hosts of *Crime and Waffles*, have this saying: "If your self-help has a leader, you're in a cult." It's definitely not a cult. What could it be?

It's probably a cult.

I make a mental note to casually check his room for clues later if he won't fess up.

A melodic *ring!* cuts into our second epic stare-off of the day.

"It's a customer," I say. "Lupe can handle it, right?"

"I'd better check," he says. "Give me a second."

"You're acting *super* sus, Dad," I say, following him out the door.

He holds up a finger and moves past the prep table toward the door to the main bakery.

"Dad! This isn't over. You—oof!"

He stops in his tracks, causing me to plow right into him.

"Really, Dad?" I go on, pushing past him. "Are you hoping to give me a concussion so I'll forget—wait, *what*?"

Standing in front of our pastry display, smiling, is my mother.

"Hey, you two," she says, in a light voice that immediately sets my nerves on edge. "Can a girl get a croissant around here?"

5

REALLY, THIS IS ALL MY FAULT.

I forgot that the spontaneous drop-in is part of Mom's signature. Like the Masterpiece Man's calling cards. Or like how this local serial killer, the Junipero Valley Killer, stole mementos from his victims. Lita Miyamoto caught them before they could wreak more havoc.

Unfortunately, even Lita couldn't stop a serial offender as sneaky as Jenn Leclair.

"Three days early. Three days!" I can hear my dad fuming after we get home. Mom and Dad had asked me to stay in my room, but I'm curled up on the floor of the hallway, listening to them argue. Just like old times.

"The airline called to say they overbooked my flight," Mom says, letting out an exasperated huff. "They offered me a first-class seat if I caught a red-eye this morning."

"When did the airline call you?" Dad asks.

I can practically hear the shrug in her voice. "A few days ago."

"Then why didn't you tell us?" Dad's voice is lower now, which is a bad sign. The calmer he seems, the more upset he actually is.

I'm not exactly calm myself. As soon as we got home, I grabbed my inhaler. Right now, I'm clutching it to my chest like a security blanket.

"And *Drew*," Dad goes on. "Did you even think about how this might affect her?"

"Drew and I are fine!" she counters.

Anger rises up inside of me. We're *fine*? Says who? I shift irritably, and my inhaler falls to the hallway floor with a loud clattering sound.

A long silence follows. Then I hear Dad suggest they move the conversation into the kitchen. After that, the voices become lower and more muffled. Clenching my teeth, I pull myself up and stalk into my room.

Is this what it's going to be like? Her showing up whenever it's convenient for her? When she's around, it's as if I'm frozen in place, afraid to move an inch until the next shoe drops. I guess I thought that, after she left, the shoes would stop dropping.

Instinctively, I grab my corkboard from under the

bed. Then, I remove a spool of red yarn and a small jar of tacks from my desk. I know I told Shrey and Trissa we would work on a crime board together, but I can prepare it, right?

After pinning up a few lengths of yarn to the corkboard, I get to work on Zora's victim profile. I have to flip past last week's profiles, but I finally reach a blank page. After referring to a few previous observations, I begin to write:

VICTIM PROFILE

NAME: Zora Mae Scurlock
AGE: 12 **RACE:** Black
EYES: Brown **HAIR:** Black
KNOWN HOBBIES: Geology and the sciences.
She checks out books on earthquakes,
even though we're not studying that in
Life Science this year. Zora is in the
Kindness Club at school, and has been
observed volunteering at more than one
school event.
CRIME COMMITTED AGAINST VICTIM: Theft
of a charm bracelet.

Pinning the profile to the center of the board, I stop and stare at it thoughtfully. I don't know why, but my thoughts keep circling back to Alix. Maybe it's the fact that, according to the national crime survey, most perpetrators are known to the victim. Or maybe it was that look they gave each other when Zora mentioned a special inscription on the charms.

I don't know Alix well, but I've always admired her casual "whatever" attitude. Even though we aren't friends, I never thought she was a jerk. Sometimes I wish I had a little more chill like her. Also, I had a true crime radar moment when Alix said that the ransom notes looked like something a "creepy killer" would send.

Maybe I should drop Lita Miyamoto into conversation to see what she says. I have to admit, having a friend I could talk to about this stuff wouldn't be *un*cool. Cool or not, though, Alix could be a suspect. I have to remember that.

After spending a few minutes checking out the student-run Instagram account ("Badgers Ahoy!"— named for our mascot), I don't come up with any posts about the locker thefts. I put my phone down, sighing, and tuck the crime board under my bed. Before long, I hear the soft padding of footsteps coming toward my bedroom.

My ears perk up nervously. It's not Dad. So . . .

"Hey, sweetie," Mom greets me in a silky voice as she opens the door and walks in. I notice that she's given up her usual khaki-and-button-down-shirt style for a more casual look. The cargo capri pants and fitted crochet top make her look thinner than she did the last time I saw her. Also, she's tan. Like *tan* tan. We're pretty white, as a family, so I imagine she's been out in the sun a lot lately. She's *definitely* been parasailing.

My body tenses. "Um, hey."

She takes a lap around my room, her eyes moving up and down the walls. There's been a lot of changes since she left, actually. It was Dad's idea to let me redecorate my room for a fresh start. Instead of dusky pink walls—Mom's choice—I'd painted my walls a cobalt blue. It was the perfect color to accent my posters and the new photos I'd added. I watch as she takes it in, wondering what she'll think when she sees that none of the pictures feature her anymore. Then, to my annoyance, she starts tidying my room.

"Mom. I'll clean it later, okay?" I say through gritted teeth.

"I don't know how you're ever going to find anything with your room this messy," she says, pushing some Post-its and Sharpies into my desk drawer.

It takes Herculean effort for me to avoid reminding her that she doesn't live here anymore. "I have a system. Okay?"

Mom stops short when she sees the framed picture of Dad and me with Lita Miyamoto. We're in front of a ceiling-high bookshelf at Twilight Books, smiling happily.

"Who's this?" she asks, pointing to Lita.

"That's Dr. Miyamoto," I remind her. "Remember? *In the Shadow of a Killer?*"

"Oh, yes. You liked that book. She's the author, right?"

It's hard to describe how infuriated I am at how she says it. Like I'm a little kid with a favorite book. She doesn't say it like a person who knows that the book completely changed my life. Or that I found out that my lifelong passion is to be a criminal profiler like Lita Miyamoto. She definitely doesn't say it like she knows that Lita was the first female profiler recognized for her work in *history*.

"Yes. I *love* that book," I respond dully. My subtle correction goes unnoticed, of course.

Mom sits at the foot of my bed. "Where did you get to meet Miss Mimato?"

"*Miya*moto," I correct her, more pointedly this time.

"When we went down to visit Grandma Joy in October there was a signing at Twilight Books." I reach under my pillow to grab my well-worn copy of *In the Shadow of a Killer* and hand it to her.

"'To my new protege,'" she reads. "'One day, you'll be signing my copy of your book. With much admiration, Lita.'" She closes the book. "That's nice."

I'm annoyed to find my voice wavers as I say, "It was one of the best days of my life. I told her all about my profiling notebooks and everything. She thinks that someone like me would be a perfect fit for the behavioral science program. Especially because there are so few women." I parrot Lita's words to the letter. "And she gave me this." I unzip my backpack and hand her the pen that Lita gave me.

"Yes," Mom says excitedly. She tosses the book aside. "The pen! Your dad told me that you're into fountain pens now. You know, there's a store in Poipu that sells Montblanc. I could get you a really nice one for your notes."

I close my eyes. She clearly doesn't realize it, but she's phrasing everything slightly wrong. "It's not about the pen being expensive," I say. In point of fact, it looks nothing like the kinds of pens you'd see in high-end stores. The black-painted brushed steel with gold writing is scuffed and nicked in a few places, like it was used. That's what makes it so special. I can imagine Lita *writing* with it.

She reads the inscription. "'It will be me.' What does that mean?"

I open my mouth to explain, but then shut it. She won't appreciate that this is a line from the letter that Lita very famously wrote to the Masterpiece Man before she caught him. Why try? "It's nothing," I say. "I'm mostly into the different kinds of ink you can get for fountain pens. They're great for drawing sku . . . er, drawing pictures."

"Well, that's great!" Mom furrows her brow, her brown eyes darting back and forth as if she's scanning for another topic. "All right, then. I guess I'll take off," she says at last. "Can I see you tomorrow? What about lunch?"

"I have school, Mom."

"You're not on winter break?"

"Nope. That ended two weeks ago."

She smacks her head. "Oh, that's right. That's why I was coming on a Saturday. Dinner?"

I scan my memory, thrilled when a totally legit excuse comes to me. "I can't. I have friends coming over. We have a new case to figure out."

She knits her brow. "A new what?"

"A case. As in, a mystery. You know, like the cyber-bully last year. Or that rabbit I found. Remember Edna and Sir Hoppington?"

Mom's expression falters. "Oh. Is that . . . usually what you do with your friends?"

"Not *usually*, but this girl needed help."

"Oh. That's nice," Mom says awkwardly. Then her eyes light up. "What if I pick you up from school tomorrow? We could grab Starbucks and I'll have you home in time for your, um, project. We can *talk*."

The word feels like a vise, squeezing me. Talk? What does that mean? Embarrassingly, my face heats up, and I feel dangerously close to crying.

"Okay, Mom."

When she finally leaves, I slump onto my bed, tears stinging my eyes. I had nearly three days to get used to the idea of her being in this house again. *Three days* that I now don't have. I'm about to completely bury my face in my pillow, when I feel something hard at my foot, and hear a *clunk* as whatever it is hits the floor.

Mom left her sunglasses. Which she'll probably want back, what with all that parasailing she's doing. It's funny that she rails on me about my room being messy when she's always leaving things everywhere. Or, she did when she *lived* here, at least.

I open the door and walk down the hall, stopping in my tracks when I hear Dad's annoyed voice again.

"Why should I be worried?" he asks.

I tiptoe down the hall stealthily, slipping the sunglasses onto the table by the front door.

"You know what I mean!" Mom protests. "She's 'solving a case'?" What does that even mean, anyway? She's twelve, Sam. She's not a criminal investigator. She's a child. And you're enabling this fantasy of hers."

I step back, stung. I'm a *child*? Engaged in a *fantasy*?

Quickly, I dart back down the hallway and into my room. It's only a few moments before I hear the front door close and Dad's footsteps at my door.

"Hey, bun."

I swat a tear from my cheek. "Hey."

"I'm really sorry. I know you weren't quite . . . ready for this."

"Three days early," I moan. "It can't be like this—her showing up whenever. It's not fair."

"I know," he says in a tired voice. "I might—well, *we* might need to talk about a more solid custodial plan."

The tears come faster as I look at him, horrified.

"What, like I spend summers with her in Kauai? I want to live with you!" In a mortifying move, I cling to him like I'm five.

"I know," he says, looking anguished. "But I promise I'll do what's best for you. Okay?"

I open my mouth to tell him what I overheard Mom say. The words keep coming back to me over and over again, invasive and cold.

I'm a *child*. My profiling and mystery-solving is a *fantasy*. She would probably think that the Plan is a fantasy too. And everything Lita told me I could do.

I wipe my face with my sleeve and ask, "Can we watch *Painted Faces* tonight? I hear it even gave Karrie and Grace nightmares."

Dad tosses his head back and laughs. "You are one of a kind. Anyone ever tell you that?"

I manage a laugh. "You, constantly."

He smiles at me and tousles my hair. "Well, I'll be ready in the living room in twenty minutes with some spaghetti marinara and a baguette."

When he closes my door, I let out a few long sobs to get them out of my system. When I've managed to pull myself together, I stand up and walk to my desk, where I notice my phone is buzzing.

Jedi Detective Agency MMS; Me, Trissa Jacobs, and 1 other

> **TRISSA:** Drew is definitely starting the crime board without us, right?
> **SHREY:** Hundo P. She's the worst.
> I laugh, typing a response.
> **ME:** I only cut lengths of yarn and made the victim profile. The rest I'm saving for you, I swear!
> **TRISSA:** Hmmm we'll see if that's really true tomorrow.
> **SHREY:** Spoiler alert: It's not true.

My smile quickly twists downward when I see the next text that comes in:

SMS; Me, Jennifer Leclair

> **JENNIFER LECLAIR:** Can't wait for tomorrow!

I throw my phone down on my bed angrily, but it doesn't help. My chest feels tight and my stomach cramps as I think of the words she used again. Feeling close to a full anxiety attack, I look around the room for something comforting.

My eyes land on my new crime board, and I set my jaw with determination.

When I catch this thief, I think, *she won't be able to say I'm living in a fantasy.* I trace my hand slowly over the corkboard and my notes. Whatever urge I might have had to bail on Zora and the mystery is totally gone now.

I need this mystery. More than ever.

6

PREETHI AGARWAL LOOKS CURIOUSLY AT me as we approach her on the blacktop, but her expression changes when she sees Shrey beside me.

OBSERVATIONS:

- Preethi quickly shoves her notebook into her bag.
- She clenches one of her crutches until her knuckles flush.
- Then she scrunches up her nose and squints, as if she just walked by a pile of poop. A fully loaded stink eye.

CONCLUSION: Shrey wasn't being dramatic.

Preethi Agarwal does *not* like him.

"Change of plans," I whisper to Shrey. "You were right about Preethi. You need to bail."

Shrey looks at Preethi, then back at me. "I *told* you," he whispers back haughtily.

Rolling my eyes, I tell him, "Your award for being right is in the mail. Now, *go*. I don't think she'll talk to me if you're here."

Shrey laughs. "You don't have to tell me twice." He jogs off with a wave and heads toward the Language Arts building.

"Preethi?" I call out, once Shrey has disappeared.

Preethi looks around in confusion. "Um, yeah?" She uses one of her forearm crutches to hoist herself up, then rests on both. *Is it my imagination, or is she still looking in the direction where Shrey ran off?*

Nope. Not my imagination. She is looking in that direction, and she does *not* look happy. At some point, I'll have to solve the mystery of Preethi's problem with Shrey, but I don't have time for that right now. I need her to answer some questions.

Mind racing, I visualize what Lita had said about interviews. In the *Game Over* podcast, Gerald and Max included Dr. Miyamoto's voice recordings from when she was hunting the Masterpiece Man. What had she said about approaching a witness again?

"Sometimes a witness will feel more inclined to talk when they feel like you know what they're going through. It might even jog their memory to share a similar story."

Yes! That's perfect.

"Can I talk to you about something?" I ask.

"Sure," Preethi says.

Lita's words flash in my mind as I formulate what to say next. "Well," I say, twisting my foot into the pavement. "The truth is, someone took my phone yesterday! And I heard the same thing might have happened to you."

Preethi stares in amazement. "Wait, really? It did—during PE! I have no idea how they knew my lock combination."

"Same!" I say, dropping my jaw theatrically.

"Whoa," Preethi replies, still looking shocked. "Jazz got something taken from *her* locker two weeks ago. But it wasn't her phone. It was a jacket."

I let my jaw drop in fake surprise, internally noting that Jazz Aguilar is the "Jasmine" Zora was talking about. "Really? Was it a nice jacket?"

Preethi looks serious. "Yeah, a Clio Love suede jacket. She got it for Christmas, I think."

"Wow, that's terrible," I say, lowering my eyes. "And

your phone was stolen last week?"

"Well, no, actually," Preethi says, making a strange face. "It was only the case. The phone was left in my locker with a bunch of other stuff. So weird." She puts her weight on her left crutch and takes her phone from her right pocket. I see a plain white iPhone without a case.

I narrow my eyes. The thief took the case and dumped the phone? That's weird. I know that iPhones are *way* more expensive than any case. Wishing I had my notebook and Lita pen out, I memorize everything Preethi said for my future profile.

"Was there something special about the case?" I ask.

"It was a Magicase," she says somberly. I can tell from her expression that this is meaningful, so I widen my eyes accordingly.

"Whoa. You must be missing that."

"You think?" Preethi says. "It was the *rose* gold, *limited*-edition Magicase with Minnie Mouse ears. They only made, like, a few hundred of them. But my mom got it for me at a conference in Anaheim." She lets out a long sigh. "My mom and I are, like, *obsessed* with them. It's kind of our thing."

Brushing aside a fleeting wish that my mom and I could bond over anything like that, I ask, "Do you have any idea who could have stolen it?"

Preethi shakes her head. "Not really. But I think that Aiden Rollerhouse kid got busted for stealing at the book fair yesterday. I overheard him talking to Vice Principal Lopez while I was in the office. Not that *I* was in trouble, of course. I was making copies for Mr. Garrison."

"Rullhausen," I correct instinctively. The *Guinness Book of World Records* thief. Could he be my first real suspect?

"My case is probably sold on eBay by now," Preethi goes on with a sigh.

I'm about to speak, when the bell rings. "Hey, can I walk with you for a second?" I ask. "There's one more thing I want to talk to you about."

"Sure." She sits back down to put her backpack on, and then starts toward the STEM building.

"Um, this is going to sound weird," I say. "But I got this note after my phone disappeared. It almost looked like one of those ransom notes in the movies. Did you get one too?" I study her face, waiting for the moment of revelation where she says: "Oops, I totally forgot to mention that ransom note!"

"That *is* weird," Preethi says. "What did it say?"

I furrow my brow as I continue to process all this information. Is it possible the thefts aren't connected after all? "Nothing," I mutter. "Maybe it was just a prank."

"If it is, it's probably your friend back there," she says.

"Shrey?" I sputter. "He would never write me a creepy note."

Preethi eyes me for a moment, her lips pursed. "If you say so. He usually throws notes *away*, I guess." She juts her chin toward the double doors to the STEM building. "Let me know if your phone turns up, okay?"

"Will do. Thanks, Preethi."

I know I was supposed to go to my Life Science class early to talk to Juan, but the bell already rang. Also, I've got so much information in my head that there might be some kind of containment failure if I don't write it down. Grasping my engraved pen, I scribble so fast that I'm sure half of what I'm writing doesn't make any sense. I can only hope I'll be able to piece together my own shorthand later. Ending my notes with a vague "Shrey + letter + Preethi = ?" I close the notebook and hurry toward class.

No Juan Madrigal, I note with a sigh as I take my seat. I gaze at the empty desk where he usually sits. *Maybe he has an early morning appointment*, I think to myself. *I can look for him after school.* With that lead temporarily out the window, I end up distracted for my morning classes. Other than actual schoolwork, I find myself doing three things on repeat:

1) Hiding my notebook inside my textbooks to continue reviewing my Preethi interview notes

2) Making a list of new inks I want for my birthday in April, since I'm already halfway through Alchemist's Dungeon

3) Composing and deleting approximately a dozen texts to my mother, canceling our coffee date.

When I get to PE, my head is swimming to the point where I actually feel kind of sick. Not my usual asthma or irritable-bowel sick, but just all over ratty. I ask my PE teacher if I can take a breather, since we always start with running sprints. I'm not lying, but I also want to check out the locker area while I can.

Coach Terry gives me the same incredulous look he usually does, but waves me off. I do note, however, that he reminds everyone to lock up their belongings because of "recent incidents."

So, the school *does* know that there's a stealing problem on campus.

It makes me wonder what information they might have so far, but I quickly brush it aside. If I'm going to solve this mystery, it's *not* going to be by snooping in the office again. That's the kind of thing that would definitely mess up the Plan.

The PE lockers at Ella Baker are lined up in front of the changing rooms. They're on the outside of the building, but there's a large chain-link fence enclosing the area that the janitors probably secure at night. During the day, I've never seen the gate closed. So, despite the changing rooms being gendered, anyone has access to the lockers.

After walking past the door to the changing room marked *Girls*, I count down the numbers until I get to locker #148. It's the one Zora told me she always uses. Every student gets a lock at the beginning of the year, assigned by the office, and we can use it where we want. But, in spite of the fact that none of the lockers are truly assigned, most people have a favorite.

As soon as I head toward locker #148, I realize why Zora picked it. It's on the top row, all the way to the right corner. A kid would have to be tall to get to the top row, and it's far enough over that there's no bench to stand on. I'm not tall like Zora, so I stand on my backpack to give myself a boost. There's no lock on there, so I open the door. Nothing.

I walk down the row, looking for a clue—any clue. As I open a few stray unlocked doors, I see them stuffed with clothes and accessories. One has several wrinkled copies of the flyer for the Winter dance that read: *GET READY FOR A WONDERLAND OF FUN!* I pick one up, roll my eyes, and stuff it back into the locker. Wandering around the corner, I start to check the bathroom entrance when I suddenly hear footsteps.

I freeze and strain my ears. Catching a glimpse of a figure moving from the locker area entrance toward the row of lockers where Zora's is, I crouch down, afraid I've been seen. But curiosity outweighs my fear, and I tiptoe back to get a better look. As soon as I recognize the figure, I gasp.

Standing on the bench, and craning a hand toward locker #148, is Alix Chang.

7

"LECLAIR!" ALIX EXCLAIMS, THROWING A hand to her chest. "Give me a heart attack, why don't you."

"Sorry," I say. "Coach Terry told me I could take a breather. Is that your . . . usual locker?"

She resumes reaching for the locker, clicks it open, and peers inside. I wait patiently for her to lie to me, but she doesn't. "Nope. It's way too high for a shorty like me. This is Zora's. Or, you know, the one she always uses. Today is her tutorial day, so she asked me to keep checking for the bracelet."

I study her. Lita says that if someone is lying, they might:

1) Fidget or gesture a lot
2) Cover their face with one or both hands
3) Look upward in the direction of their dominant hand.

I'm not sure if Alix is right or left-handed, but she doesn't look up in either direction. She does put one hand to her pale golden-toned cheek as she speaks, however. And she fidgets with a bracelet on her arm—the same one, with sun- and heart-shaped charms that was so similar to Zora's.

Hmmm. Fidgeting.

"Hey, nice sticker, by the way," Alix says, pointing to the binder that I'm clutching in front of my notebook.

"Which one?" I ask, without moving to look at it.

"The *Legend of Korra* sticker. It's pretty much my favorite show ever." Alix grins. "But I thought you were into horror movies or something?"

"True crime," I clarify. I watch her reaction to see if there are any hints that she could be among my people. You know, the "preternaturally fascinated by murder" people.

Alix merely looks at me right back, as if she's trying to figure something out, too. "That would explain all the skulls," she says.

My face reddens. "That's fair. I'm mostly into doc-umentaries," I go on. "Do you ever listen to podcasts?"

"Of course I do," Alix says, smirking. I wait for her to elaborate. But she only gives me an inscrutable smile. Then she hops down and faces me, putting one hand on her hip. "So, are you having an asthma attack?"

I blink at her, surprised. "Not an attack; just feeling a little under the weather," I explain. "You remembered I have asthma?"

"Well, yeah. I had Ms. Garcia with you at Cypress Grove. You were absent, what, two months that year?" She slumps down and leans back on one arm, her other hand toying with her messy bun.

"Just about," I say, sitting down on the other end of the bench. "But that was only because I got pneumonia."

Suddenly I feel like I've been driven off track. Wasn't I supposed to be finding out if Alix is the thief? How did she talk me into this corner? I bite my lip, thinking of the best way to turn the subject back to Zora's missing bracelet, and the suspicious look they shared yesterday. Maybe if I bring up Shrey and Trissa, that could be an opening . . .

"You called me 'Leclair,'" I point out. "It's funny, I call myself that, but nobody else does. Maybe Shrey sometimes."

Alix rubs her belly. "Maybe it's because I'm obsessed with your dad's pastries."

I laugh. "Also fair."

"Speaking of Shrey, though . . ." Alix begins.

Wait . . .

"Is he into Zora or what?"

Okay, it was officially the worst idea ever to bring up Shrey. "Umm," I hedge.

"Because she definitely likes him," Alix says. "Or, I'm pretty sure. She keeps, like, randomly bringing him up in conversations."

"Wait, *really*?" My jaw actually drops like I'm a cartoon. But, despite the weird feeling I had yesterday when he bailed to talk to Zora, I don't feel upset about it. I mostly feel excited to tell Shrey this new tidbit. "She brings him up? Like by name?"

Alix's lips curl upward into a satisfied smile. "So, he *does* like her."

"Um, I didn't say that . . ."

She presses her lips together. "You sounded excited. Dead giveaway."

Yikes, is *Alix* the profiler now? What can I say other than "um" right now?

"Umm."

She laughs. "Hey, I get it. You want to keep his secret. Honor among bros, and all. But it doesn't have to be a secret if he asks her to the dance. I'm telling you without *telling* you—she will say yes." She gives me an exaggerated wink.

"Understood," I say with a nod.

"Okay," Alix says. "I'm glad we had this chat." She gets up from the bench and pats me on the back as she walks out of the locker area, leaving me wondering what the heck just happened.

When I walk into the library, the book fair is bustling and Mr. Covacha has a line at the register.

"Drew, can you sign in and manage the counter?" he calls out.

"Will do!" I call back, glad for a chance to check the volunteer binder right away.

As soon as I drop my backpack, I grab the binder, flipping to the section that lists lunchtime helpers. Volunteers are the only kids (other than me, of course) who are allowed behind the library counter. Any of them would have the means to leave notes for Zora. It's not like anyone couldn't sneak behind the counter to access the holds, but it can't hurt to check.

My eyes scan down the log, seeing a few names I recognize. Each semester, new kids come into the gig, so I noticed a new group of names as I flipped to the weeks after winter break. Nothing really jumps out at me until I get to Thursday.

Emma Cruz

As in, Emma Cruz, one of my three former tormentors. Who I literally noticed getting back to her rude

73

ways *yesterday*. I've never heard accounts of her stealing, but she's nasty enough to play a prank. Also, I'm not convinced yet that the thefts are linked. But Emma is certainly an interesting suspect.

I jot her name down in my notebook and shove it back into my bag. Then I return the binder to its spot and head to the front counter. When the book fair rush finally dies down, Mr. Covacha walks over to me holding out a small pink paper square.

"Drew," he says hurriedly. "Someone from the office just handed me this a few minutes ago. Sorry, it got too busy for me to give it to you right away."

I look at him, alarmed, as he hands me a pass. All it says is *Drew Leclair*, with a checkmark next to the selection marked *Office* for location, and *Immediately* for time. What could they be sending a pass for? I consider the options, but none of them amount to good news.

"I don't have to go if you still want me here," I offer.

"If they need you, they need you," Mr. Covacha says. "Why don't you take your bag? It's almost the end of the period."

"All right," I say miserably.

As I walk to the office, my mind races. Is the pass from Vice Principal Lopez? Have I done something that could get me in trouble?

Gulping, I open the back door to the office. I never felt this nervous walking into the office before the Ella Baker Shade mystery. Since I broke into the file room, Mr. Lopez has been having "check-ins" with me more often. And Ms. Marika, our school secretary, definitely doesn't trust me anymore. I don't blame them. That day, I was acting way more like a perpetrator than a (future world-renowned) criminal profiler.

I walk down the hallway, past the counseling office, and round the corner toward the front office. When I do, my heart stops.

Standing there, yet again, is my mother.

"Hi, kiddo," she says brightly. "I'm here to take you to that dentist appointment." She gives me a conspiratorial smile, like we're both in on her lie.

Because of *course* she took my forced interest in coffee yesterday as an invitation to pick me up early. My hand instinctively clenches into a fist as I attempt to smile back at her.

Leaving early means I can't hang around to try to catch Emma in the library during lunch. It also means I can't talk to Zora during Core, or try to find Jazz and Juan after school. *Or* tell Shrey and Trissa about the library volunteer connection.

After talking to Preethi today, and seeing Emma's

name on that log, I'd started to feel like this mystery was more than a favor to Shrey. I was starting to feel *excited*. But now, that sense of momentum is shriveling—like the sad, half-dead peace lily on Ms. Marika's desk.

Having Mom around is going to be a problem.

8

AS I SIP MY TRIPLE-PUMP vanilla Frappuccino and look at pictures of Mom's new condo, I find myself wondering two things: (1) Is it possible for a person to be more clueless than Mom? and (2) Would Dad be really mad if I used his credit card to book her on a flight back to Kauai?

I *should* be able to be honest with Mom about how furious I am with her right now. Especially since I've been working on the whole holding-in-my-emotions issue these past few months. But, every time I try to open my mouth, I can't do it.

Instead, the anger churns in my stomach, looking for a way out. It's uncomfortable to say the least—especially after the Frappuccino. Along with high-fat food, my doctor says to lay off dairy. But it's really hard.

My favorite foods can be so comforting, even if they cause me pain afterward. It feels unfair, like I'm getting punished for eating something that every other kid gets to enjoy.

Turns out, being a detective while also having anxiety . . . kinda sucks.

Lita Miyamoto says that we can't have justice *or* change without accountability. Which is a fancy way of saying that Mom will never change if she doesn't understand that she's hurting me. Am I basically causing Mom's terrible behavior by staying quiet? Maybe this Frappuccino won't turn on me if I *say* something.

Still, when her eyes lock on mine and she asks me if I like her new across-a-whole-ocean house, I can only say, "Mm-hmm. The condo looks nice."

"I can't wait for you to visit," she gushes. "The pool has a slide!"

Okay. I have to admit that a pool slide is pretty sweet. But I can't bring myself to offer her any more enthusiasm right now.

"Sounds fun."

Mom frowns a little and pockets her phone. Clearly, this isn't the excited "Omigod, a *pool slide*?!" response she was hoping for.

"So, what time are you usually off school again?" she

asks, sipping her nonfat latte.

"A little before two," I say. "But only because it's an early-release day."

"So I didn't get you *too* early, then." She smiles triumphantly.

Lita's point about accountability rings in my ears. "Um, actually, Mom . . ." I begin.

Her phone cuts me off, ringing loudly. I look down and see Mr. Clark's goofy face bobbing up and down on the screen. Awesome.

"Oops!" she says with a laugh. "Hold that thought, sweetie." She grabs her phone, swipes up delicately, and moves a few feet away from our table.

I take the free moment to text Shrey and Trissa.

Jedi Detective Agency MMS; Me, Trissa Jacobs, and 1 other

> **ME:** Hey, I had to leave school early. Can one of you find Juan Madrigal after school to ask him about the thefts? He was absent this morning but he might be there now. Also, Jazz Aguilar. Preethi told me that she's the Jasmine we're looking for.

It's only a moment before Shrey answers. I glance at

the clock on my phone. Wow, it's already, like, 1:20. He's probably on his way to his last class.

> **SHREY:** These are not the Jasmines you're looking for.
> **ME:** Ha-ha, Obi Wan.
> **TRISSA:** 😂
> **TRISSA:** I can talk to Jazz no problem. I'm hanging out after school anyway.
> **SHREY:** I'll take Juan. Hey, why did you leave early? Are you sick?
> **ME:** No. I'll fill you in later.
> **TRISSA:** Intriguing!

I hastily pocket my phone when I see Mom coming back.

"Hey, sweetie!" she says breathlessly. "What were we talking about?"

I take a breath. It's now or never. "We were talking about you picking me up early today." Before I can lose my nerve, I go on. "It's just that, um, you didn't ask me first. I had a quiz today, and a project in technology class. Now I'll have to make those up." I'm way overplaying my day, but I don't want to tell her all about the locker thefts and ransom notes. Or that my tight schedule included questioning my fellow students. Not after what she said to Dad.

I brace myself for her response. She'll probably say something about me being ungrateful, or that I need to act more like a kid. She'll say—

"Oh, honey, I'm so sorry."

Whoa. Not that.

"What?" I reply, choking a little.

"I didn't think. I assumed you'd be relieved to leave school early."

"That's . . . not me," I say carefully.

She puts up her hands. "I get it. It won't happen again. I guess I have to keep reminding myself that you're not me. You *like* academics."

"You didn't like school?"

"Well, I ditched class a lot," she confesses. "Don't tell your dad I told you that. Anyway, I'm glad that you're so dedicated to school."

I let out a long sigh, feeling the weight of the conversation slip from my shoulders. "You're not mad?" I ask. "That I didn't want to get picked up early?"

"Never," she says, reaching forward to tuck my hair behind one ear.

Ugh. I'll fix that later.

"Thanks, Mom. And I promise I'll be more available

this weekend."

"I hope so," she says. "You're why I'm here!"

Instinctively, warmth spreads across my stomach. But not in a bad way. Is it possible that I just had a not-terrible conversation with my mother?

We sit, sipping our drinks, for another forty-five minutes. And . . . it really *isn't* so bad. Now that the condo conversation is over, she mostly asks me about school, my new friends, and my trip to see Grandma Joy. She even asks for more details about the Lita Miyamoto signing *and* gets her name right. Then, we look at all the inks I'm obsessed with on Etsy. For a few minutes there, I think she might be making an effort to get to know me better. Maybe then she'll understand how important mysteries are to me, not like some childish hobby but a *real* passion.

"And then, she told me that I could *actually* become a profiler," I gush. "I have to go through the FBI academy, of course, and I definitely need to get my asthma under control. I'd have to live in Quantico, Virginia, for a while to train, but that could be okay."

"Wow! That's very impressive," she says. "You know, I still have a trust set up for you from Grandpa Roy's estate that you could use for college."

My eyes pop. "Wait, what?" I knew Mom had a trust

fund. It was probably how she was able to skip off to Kauai without a job lined up. But I didn't know that included me.

"Of course!" Mom says. "Your dad and I are sharing costs, but we have a trust set up that you can use for education. Or to travel the world! It would be your choice."

My choice? Suddenly, I can see the Plan legitimately playing out in front of me. I try to stay cool. "Did you use your trust fund for college?"

She laughed. "Only for a year. It wasn't for me. But I'm glad you're interested. Look, I know I was a little weird last night when you told me about your . . . case. But your father set me straight and told me how important this is for your future. I want you to know I'm willing to help in any way I can."

OBSERVATIONS:

- Mom smiles at me, and doesn't break eye contact.
- She's talking about paying for college.
- She hasn't said that the Plan is a fantasy, or that I'm kidding myself.

CONCLUSION: Is Mom actually being supportive right now?

Speechless, I gaze at her. Her words sound great, but I keep waiting for her support to turn into something else. Is this for real, or one of her fake-outs?

"Hey, can I get a pumpkin loaf? I didn't eat lunch today." A pumpkin loaf is definitely not an approved stomach-happy food but I kind of want to see what she'll say. Normally, if I pick out an unhealthy meal, she'll look super obviously at my midsection, or point out every calorie and gram of fat in what I picked.

"Sure, sweetie! Here's a twenty."

Okay, what's going on?

Is this Bizzarro Mom?

I'm about to ask for a cake pop to wash down the pumpkin loaf, when I feel a buzz at my hip. I bring my phone back up to check it.

Jedi Detective Agency MMS; Me, Trissa Jacobs, and 1 other

TRISSA: Shrey couldn't find Juan, but we talked to Jazz. Her jacket did get stolen. She used her lock for sure. But no ransom notes.

"What is it?" Mom asks when she sees me frowning at the screen.

"My friends," I say. "No problem."

"It didn't look like 'no problem,'" she points out. "Does this have anything to do with the Wonderland dance?"

Wait, *what*? How is my mother, who only yesterday didn't know I was in school, suddenly aware of the Wonderland dance? It's like she's got some kind of radar for things I have zero interest in.

"Dustin asked me if it was coming up," she explains, blushing. "And I saw the posters when I picked you up today."

Ah. Of course, Mr. Clark knows about the dance. He worked at Ella Baker up until a few months ago. You know, counseling needy kids and then dating their parents.

"It's not exactly my thing," I say carefully.

"I thought you might be going with Shrey," Mom goes on.

"He's probably going with a date," I reply. For some reason, it occurs to me at that moment that Shrey and I had made plans to avoid the dance together. I mean, it was only a plan involving pizza and a replay of *Super Paper Mario*. But, still.

That nagging feeling of sadness hits me again like a quick knife to the gut. What *is* this? Am I bothered by Shrey and Zora getting together, or aren't I? Honestly, I wish Mom hadn't brought it up at all . . .

My phone buzzes again.

Jedi Detective Agency MMS; Me, Trissa Jacobs, and 1 other

SHREY: But there's something else!

"Hold on a second," I tell Mom, giving the text chain my full attention.

ME: Which is . . . ??
TRISSA: God, Shrey, vague much?
ME: You're killing me. WHAT IS IT?

"Do you still want that pumpkin loaf?" Mom asks.

"I should get home, if that's okay," I tell her.

She frowns but says, "All right, sweetie. Whatever you need. Let's head back home."

"Thanks, Mom," I murmur, watching as the three dots dance on my screen. I love my friends, but they are literally murdering me right now. After what feels like an eternity, a response finally pops up.

TRISSA: Sorry! Shrey and I walked over to the PE area with Jazz and guess who we saw skulking around, poking her head in everyone's lockers?

SHREY: EMMA CRUZ!

9

I'M HOPPING FROM FOOT TO foot with excitement by the time Shrey and Trissa arrive at my house a few hours later. Since Mom dropped me off, I'd already begun preparing for our night of crime boarding. The nearly blank corkboard sits in the living room, along with my tacks, the red yarn, note cards, and a variety of colored Sharpies and highlighters.

It's go time.

"Cereal?" Trissa asks when she arrives a few minutes after Shrey.

I jerk a thumb toward the kitchen. "You know where to find it. But, fair warning, Dad hasn't been buying as much of the sugary stuff lately."

For some reason, this jogs my memory back to my observations yesterday: smiling more, vague mentions of getting his life back, and now healthier cereal options? With all the Mom drama, I'd totally forgotten to look for clues for this maybe–love interest. Now that I'm thinking about it, is Dad *actually* out with friends tonight? I make a mental note to ask him later.

Speaking of a laundry list of drama, I still have to tell Shrey what Alix told me. And I have to tell both of them about Mom coming early. Which I really should do first.

"Okay, friends, let's start with the crime board!" I announce.

Or . . . not.

"Wait, what happened to you telling us why you left school?" Trissa accuses. Cereal threatens to slosh over the edge of her bowl as she walks toward the couch, but she manages to contain it.

"Yeah!" Shrey backs her up.

I look forlornly at the crime board. "Fine," I say. "On one condition. Tell me about Emma first, because I'm dying to know what you saw."

Trissa swallows a huge bite and then says, "So, we talked to Jazz after school—"

"The notes you sent us helped, by the way," Shrey interrupts. "Very thorough."

"Yes," Trissa agrees. "Anyhow, like Preethi, she didn't get any messages. But she did say that other valuable stuff was left in the locker—as in, it was taken out of her jacket pockets and dumped. Sort of like Zora said with her other stuff. We asked Jazz to show us where her locker was, and that's where we saw Emma."

"Was she carrying a lock-picking kit, or looking extra thief-y?" I ask hopefully.

"Thief-y?" Trissa repeats with a giggle.

"We only saw her opening a bunch of the lockers," Shrey tells me. "Not sure if that's 'thief-y' or not."

"Okay," I say, letting out a sigh. "I was hoping for more of a smoking gun, but I think that still puts her toward the top of our suspect list. Especially because—and this part I forgot to text you—Emma is the Thursday lunch volunteer at the library."

"Wait, really?" Shrey asks. "I thought it was Brian."

"New volunteer cycle, remember?" I say. "And you probably missed Emma today while you were off looking for me at lunch. Mr. Covacha changes it up at the semester mark, which was technically the end of last week. I only started so early because my schedule changed after I got . . . ummm . . ."

"Fired from your office TA job for breaking and entering?" Shrey offers.

I narrow my eyes into slits.

Trissa looks between us, concern marring her usually

bright expression. "Anyway," she says firmly, "that tracks about the semester change, but why didn't we see her today? Also known as *Thursday*."

I tap a finger to my chin thoughtfully. "Interesting. And suspicious." Now that they're in full mystery mode, I wonder if I can steer them away from other subjects. "So . . . crime board?"

"Nice try," Shrey says.

"All right, *fine*," I moan. "I left school because my mom picked me up."

"Wait, like, she just showed up at school out of the blue?" Trissa asks, visibly horrified.

"She actually came last night," I grumbled. "Three days early."

Shrey looks mad, which I expected. "And you were going to tell us *when*?"

"I'm really sorry," I say, clasping my hands together to plead with him. "She came to the bakery and then you all were texting about the mystery, and I . . . I just wanted to focus on that instead of Mom."

"All right," he says in an irritated voice.

"I mean, it's kind of your business," Trissa says, giving Shrey a pointed look.

"Except when keeping secrets makes Drew do things. You know, like *profile* us?"

"Oh, come on, Malhotra," Trissa cuts him off. "She profiled me, too, and it's not like I'm mad. Quit being a drama king."

"A *drama* king?!" Shrey barks, his ears reddening.

"I said what I said," she retorts. She's setting her jaw defiantly, but looks way more upset than she's letting on with her words.

OBSERVATIONS:

- Trissa is getting the same funny look on her face that she had a few minutes ago.
- She's looking between us.

CONCLUSION: Something is bothering Trissa, and it might have something to do with me and Shrey.

My mind races with ideas to cut the tension, when the perfect segue pops into my head.

"ZORA SCURLOCK LIKES SHREY!" I shout.

A stunned silence follows. Then, in slow motion, Trissa's mouth curls into an amused smile and Shrey gives me a look like he might faint. I'm not sure if I said it to keep them from fighting, or to make Shrey stop being upset with me. Either way, it sure seems to have worked.

"W-what?!" he sputters.

I can't seem to lower the volume of my voice as I go on. "ZORA SCURLOCK LIKES YOU AND SHE WANTS YOU TO ASK HER TO THE DANCE!"

Shrey's face goes through about a dozen emotions, but lands on skepticism. "Wait. Are you only saying this so I won't be mad at you about keeping the mom stuff from us?"

"Yes, obviously! But it's also true."

Shrey's emotions rewind to bug-eyed shock. "What?"

I'm relieved to see Trissa relax back onto the couch, arms behind her head and looking ready for a show—no sign of still being upset. "Go on, Ms. Leclair," she drawls.

"Okay, so remember how I texted you all that I saw Alix looking in Zora's usual locker?" I ask. "Well, I was trying to think of a way to ask her about the bracelet without it being weird. Then I brought you up, Shrey. And then Alix was like, 'Speaking of Shrey—'"

"Speaking of Shrey!" Shrey repeats, wringing his hands.

"She straight-up asked if you liked Zora. I didn't say anything, but then she said that she was pretty positive that Zora likes you, because she brings up your name a lot. I'm not sure about that. I mean, I bring up Lita Miyamoto's name a lot and I don't want to marry her or anything. Although if my *dad* wanted to marry her, that'd be awesome, because then we could be this crime-fighting family and—"

"DREW!" Shrey exclaims in anguished anticipation.

"Sorry! Yeah, Alix said she was *sure* that if you ask Zora to the dance, she'll say yes." I break off, taking a deep breath after my rambling story.

Shrey collapses back against the couch, looking like he got hit by a bus or something. Or maybe a thousand somethings.

"So . . . are you going to ask her to the dance?" Trissa asks.

"Wait, I have to ask her to the dance?"

Trissa and I exchange an exasperated look. "Yes!" we cry in unison.

"I think dances are a total waste of time," I say. "But even I think you should ask her. You like her, she likes you. We're in seventh grade. It's not like we're allowed to go on dates or anything. A dance is literally your best chance if you want her to be your girlfriend."

"Yeah?" he says nervously.

"It's basically science," I confirm. I wait to feel that twinge I felt when I thought about Shrey going to the dance, but it doesn't come. So, maybe I *am* happy for him? I don't know. Feelings are weird and, most days, I don't want any part of them.

"Wow," he says. "I guess I'm asking Zora Scurlock to the Wonderland dance."

Trissa squeals, grabbing his arm and squeezing. "I told you that deodorant was fresh."

That's the line that does us in. All *three* of us bust up laughing.

Then, predictably, we spend the next hour plotting the best way for Shrey to ask Zora to the dance. Normally I'd be annoyed, but I'd rather talk about Zora than my mom, so it's all good. After we eat, I manage to direct their attention back to the task at hand: our mystery.

"My friends!" I exclaim, smacking my pointer toward the blank corkboard. "Our mission is simple. We have three very similar crimes, and a possible fourth and fifth."

"Oh!" Trissa interjects. "I forgot to mention this with the whole Emma reveal. I talked to Liz today, and she said it was the same deal. After her Harper Berry palette went missing, there was even *cash* left behind. That's why she wasn't a hundred percent sure it was stolen at first."

I move the name "Liz Davis" over to the "Confirmed

Victims" section.

"All the confirmed thefts are from girls so far," Shrey points out. "So maybe Juan wasn't one of the victims? I guess we won't know if he fits the pattern until we talk to him. Hopefully he'll be back tomorrow."

"Coach Terry told us to make sure we locked up our stuff because of personal items going missing," I point out. "So, there could be even more victims than we know."

"Also, they relaxed the rules about mixed-gender groups hanging out by the lockers this year," Trissa says. "The changing rooms are still separate, but they did that push when we were in sixth grade to make things more gender neutral. Honestly, I'm surprised they didn't do it sooner. There's more than one kid at Ella Baker with 'they' pronouns."

"That's a good point," I say. "The lockers are outside, so pretty much anyone could access them anyway. Connor hung out with me when I was out of PE a few weeks ago, and Vice Principal Lopez just waved at us."

"Well, whoever it is, it's got to be the same thief, right?" Shrey asks.

"Maybe," I say thoughtfully. "But I'm not sure. The signature is different. Only Zora is getting ransom notes so far."

Trissa blinks. "Sure, but there's also the second signature."

"Second signature?" I repeat.

"The thief takes one item and leaves other items of value behind," Trissa explains. "I mean, maybe that's more of a modus operandi, but still. What are the odds that two thieves are acting on their own with that same move? It's super weird to leave money behind from the thing you're stealing—or to return a phone because you only want the case."

Beaming at her, I say, "Wow. You're absolutely right. With that, we should organize what we have so far to see if there are any *more* connections."

"Who are our suspects so far?" Shrey asks.

"Our book thief, Aiden Rullhausen," I say, tacking a printed picture to the board. "Preethi overheard him talking to Vice Principal Lopez. It sounds like he might have a history of theft."

I grab the half-sheet of paper on which I've written Aiden's mini-suspect profile.

OFFENDER PROFILES

NAME: Aiden (middle name?) Rullhausen
MEANS: Has access to lockers, and is

tall enough to reach locker #148
PREVIOUS OFFENSES: Stole a Guinness
Book of World Records from the book fair
MOTIVE: Unknown, maybe an impulse to
steal?
OPPORTUNITY: All students have access to
the PE lockers during school hours
COUNTERPOINT: The confirmed thefts
include a sparkly cell phone case, a
suede jacket, makeup, and a bracelet.
Previous observations have not indicated
that this fits with Aiden's usual
personal style.

"Then there's Alix," I state, pinning another picture
and sheet to the board.

NAME: Alix Xiuying Chang
MEANS: Has access to the PE locker area
and knows Zora's usual locker.
MOTIVE: Unknown. Could possibly have to
do with the look she shared with Zora?
OPPORTUNITY: As her best friend, Alix
might know when Zora places the library
holds. She could have easily stolen the

bracelet and snuck behind the counter to
tuck the notes in her books.
COUNTERPOINT: She is too short to easily
reach Zora's locker. Also, why would she
steal Zora's bracelet when she has an
identical one?

"And . . . *Emma*," I finish with a flourish.

NAME: Emma Marin Cruz
MEANS: Has access to the PE locker area
and library holds area.
MOTIVE: Emma has a history of cruel
behavior. Could the thefts and notes be
a big joke to her?
OPPORTUNITY: Could have easily placed
the notes in Zora's books during her
volunteer shift.
COUNTERPOINT: None. Emma is basically a
fire-breathing she-beast.

"Except this counterpoint," Shrey says, scribbling on
the paper with a lavender Sharpie. "'Drew hates Emma
and might be biased toward her as a suspect,'" he reads
aloud.

I make a *psshaw* sound. "Me, biased? I don't think so. All the evidence clearly puts her in our top suspect position. Do you remember when I told you two about the Masterpiece Man? Well, on the *Game Over* podcast, they aired his confession tapes. He didn't actually resell any of the artwork he stole, or display it in his house. He stole because he didn't think the museums and private owners *deserved* the art. He wanted to take it away more than he wanted to have it. Doesn't that sound like an Emma move?"

Trissa says, nodding at the profiles thoughtfully, "Of the three, she's the most likely."

"You're not wrong," Shrey relents. He digs a paper out of his messenger bag. "I made a list of all the dates of the thefts. That helps, right?"

I grab the note and pin it up even though I'd made my own list. "This is perfect, Shrey. Thank you."

"And I drew pictures of the missing items," Trissa adds. She pins up a small sketch of the phone case, jacket, and bracelet. "I already checked a bunch of places online like eBay and Mercari to see if they were listed for sale." She rattles off a few more secondhand groups and sites. "Nothing, though."

"You two really came prepared," I say. "I'm impressed."

"So, what do we do next?" Trissa asks.

"I'm hoping to see Juan tomorrow if he's not absent again. We already confirmed Preethi and Jazz, and I'd like if he fits in with this. Oh, by the way," I add, looking at Shrey, "what's *up* with you and Preethi? She really doesn't like you."

"I know, right?!" Shrey exclaims. "I have no idea what I did, but she's been giving me these mean looks for almost the whole year."

Trissa sighs. "Another mystery."

"But one for another day," I say firmly. "There are too many missing pieces in this mystery so far. We have a lot of work ahead of us."

"Including interrogating your least-favorite person," Shrey says.

"Eh, she's my second or third least favorite," I reply.

"Who knows?" Trissa says excitedly. "Maybe she'll just confess." She puts a dramatic hand to her forehead. "I do declare! It was *me*!"

"Why does Emma have a Southern accent?" Shrey asks, laughing.

"It felt right," Trissa says.

I look between them, buzzing with excitement. Who knows? Maybe Trissa is right. If all goes according to plan, this mystery could be solved before we know it.

10

LITA MIYAMOTO USES THIS WORD to describe the feeling right before you question your best suspect. It's *fängenfreude*, which very roughly translates from German as "joy of the catch." It's the perfect word to describe the feeling I'm having right now. Because, could there *be* a better suspect to take down than Emma Cruz?

The next morning, Shrey, Trissa, and I made it our mission to find Emma first, since I share Life Science class with Juan. After finding out from a reluctant Brie and Alicia that Emma was decorating for the dance before school, we finally spot her in the multipurpose room.

"Where on earth are we going to store a ten-foot yeti until next Tuesday?" Emma is yelling at Olivia Campos, who I recognize from my Core class.

"Maybe backstage?" Olivia offers.

I blink at Shrey and Trissa, confused for a moment. A *yeti*?

Shrey nods toward the right-hand wall of the multipurpose room. Leaning against the wall is a giant, cartoonish wooden yeti. His midsection is covered in cotton-ball fluff and he has a goofy grin—less like the abominable snowman from the Matterhorn, and more like Bumble from those old Claymation Christmas movies.

As I'm about to move toward Emma and fulfill my *fängenfreude* dreams, we see a familiar face duck out from behind the yeti—Connor Brady.

"Connor!" Trissa says, waving.

"Hey! Are you here to help with the Wonderland dance prep?" Connor asks.

"No," I tell him, lowering my voice. "We're actually here on . . . business."

Connor grins. "Say no more, Detective Leclair. Sorry I haven't seen you guys at lunch much these days. Brian and I have been super busy rehearsing."

"Oohh. 'Brian and I,'" Trissa trills, ever the shipper. "That sounds official."

Connor covers his light brown cheeks with his hands in mock embarrassment. "Maybe. Whatever, Jacobs!"

Trissa giggles and smacks him playfully.

"So, will I see all of you at the dance?" Connor asks. He has a starry-eyed expression as he adds, "Brian is my date."

"Looks like I'm going," Shrey tells him with an embarrassed shrug.

"Me too!" Trissa pipes up.

"What about you?" Connor asks me.

I bite my lip. Could Mom be right? Is this dance supposed to be something I care about? Am I this socially deficient kid who doesn't get that this is a huge milestone?

"You'd better be there," Connor tells me in a warning voice.

"Uhh . . ." I hedge.

"Connor!" an eighth-grade boy calls out, saving me. "Can you help me with the banner?"

Connor's eyes follow to where the boy is pointing, at a large banner on the ground by the stage. "Okay, I've got to go, but I will see you at the dance. *All* of you, right?" He looks at me.

"I guess?" I say.

"Really?" Trissa cries out happily. "Yay!"

Yikes. Do I *have* to go now?

I'm about to direct us back toward Emma—or

anything that will get us off the dance topic—when a harried-looking Kenzie Perl suddenly pushes past us.

She walks up to our counseling secretary, Mr. Crohner, and states, "We need to keep this in a *secure* location."

Mr. Crohner looks as confused as I do. "What?" he asks.

"The DJ station!" Kenzie says, gesturing irritably at a large black box with a speaker. "We can't just leave it out. Things get stolen that way."

My ears perk up at the reference to stealing. Kenzie is another kid who lives in Clearview Heights, like Zora. She's probably the richest kid in our class. Her father is the creator of SETEC, the most used internet company in the East Bay area. Honestly, I'm surprised that Kenzie doesn't go to private school. She seems like the type.

Kenzie would have a lot to tempt a thief. Could she be another victim? I become so engrossed in staring at Kenzie while she berates poor Mr. Crohner that I almost don't react when Shrey elbows me.

"Hey," he whispers, gesturing toward Emma. Now that she's alone, her eyes have moved on from the giant snow monster and landed squarely on us.

"What are *you* doing here?" Emma asks sourly, crossing her arms and displaying clear hostility in her body language. "None of you are on the dance committee."

"We're here to talk to you." I manage to keep my voice totally even—*not* like someone who can recall her taunts like they're playing in surround sound.

Emma rolls her eyes and gestures to Kenzie, Olivia, and the other volunteers. "We only have one dance for our entire seventh grade year. The eighth graders get *two*," she says pointedly. "So, I'm kind of busy."

Trissa nods to the left of the stage and says, "This will only take a minute. It's about the *lockers*." She says the last part quietly, but Emma clearly hears.

"All right," she says.

The three of us trade a look of surprise. Is it possible that she's going to confess?

Emma follows us off to the side of the stage, where we're more or less alone. "So, is this about what was stolen?" she asks, tapping a foot. "Look, I don't need any help, okay? I can find my own stuff."

"Wait, *what*?" I ask. This conversation is leaving me more confused with every word.

"That's why you're here, isn't it?" she asks. She stops looking between all three of us and rounds on me. "Brie overheard you talking to Preethi. She said someone stole your phone?"

OBSERVATIONS:

- Emma is being weirdly accommodating right now.
- She's talking to me like we share an experience.

CONCLUSION: Emma was another *victim* of the thefts. Not our top suspect. That must have been why she was looking in the lockers yesterday. To find her missing item.

Still . . . it's *Emma Cruz*.

Could she be trying to throw me off track? I study her face for the usual indicators. Direct eye contact, no face touching . . . but she is being pretty vague.

"Anyway," she goes on, pointing at Shrey and Trissa, "then I saw *you two* in the locker area yesterday and I figured you knew about me too."

"What did they take from your locker?" I ask.

"My backpack," she replies.

"Like . . . your full backpack?" Shrey asks. He shrugs off his own plain black canvas bag and points at it.

Emma regards Shrey's bag, discolored in several places and covered with nerdy patches, as if it's a cockroach. "Um, no," she tells us. "It was my red *leather* Swoon and Swank backpack purse."

"Swoon and Swank?" Trissa repeats, looking impressed. "Whoa. Did you get the Avengers print one?"

Emma laughs derisively. "No. Plain red is more my style." Then she gives me a hard look. "Did someone even *take* your phone? Or are you being Nosy Drew again?"

Indignation courses through me. I'm about to retort, when Shrey gets there first.

"Hey, Emma. Don't forget that Drew being 'nosy' is the whole reason we don't have Ella Baker Shade after us anymore," Shrey snaps. "Ethan was the reason your friend Alicia missed a week of school, wasn't he? After he made that embarrassing post?"

"Fine," Emma says. "Look, if you find my backpack I don't care *how* nosy you are."

It's the nicest thing she could possibly say, so I ignore the rest and pull out my notebook. "Okay, then. When was your bag stolen?"

"Tuesday," Emma says. "During PE."

"And was there anything left behind?" Trissa asks carefully. "Like something of value from the purse, money . . . or a *note* or something?"

Emma's brows pinch together at the center. "Yeah. How did you know?"

I look excitedly at Emma. Did she get a ransom note?

"Everything from my purse was, like, *dumped* out," she says. "I had some cash and my phone. But that was the weird thing. Everything from the bag was still in my locker."

"The thief left behind everything but your purse?" Trissa repeats, eyeing me.

"Yeah," Emma says. "I was actually sort of annoyed. I have my mom's way-old iPhone six. If they were going to take my bag, they could have at least taken that ratty, cracked-screen phone so I could get a new one."

"Don't take this the wrong way, but couldn't you have bought a new phone instead of the bag?" I blurt. I know it's not a polite question, but I'm not super in the mood to watch my manners with Emma.

Emma's face softens uncharacteristically. "My grandpa got me that bag. He doesn't even have that much money. He just likes to spoil me, I guess. When I saw that it was gone from my locker and someone just . . . dumped it out?" She trails off, rubbing her arm.

I know that look. Zora had it too, when we talked to her the other day. It wasn't just that something was stolen, it was that the thief practically ransacked the victims' lockers. I may not like Emma, but I understand how that feels. It reminds me of when my mom goes on one of her cleaning binges in my room, and just dumps all this stuff that's really important to me in the drawers. It's like having your space violated.

"Anyhow," she says. "It's not like my family is the Perls. I can't just get a new bag."

All of us glance over at Kenzie, who's still barking orders at everyone.

"Speaking of which, I'd better get back," Emma says, regarding Kenzie with annoyance. "Kenzie's dad paid for all of the Wonderland dance stuff, and she's acting like our boss."

We say a quick goodbye and watch as Emma rejoins the eighth graders, presumably to solve the yeti problem.

"Well, there goes our top suspect," Trissa says in a low voice.

"Or she's lying," Shrey points out.

"We'll have to keep investigating to confirm her story," I say with a sigh. "But, if she's *not* lying, Emma is one of the victims—not our perp."

"I can't believe she got to pick a Swoon and Swank and didn't get the Avengers print," Trissa mutters. "It has chibi Lokis on it!"

"So that makes *six* thefts in two weeks, right?" Shrey

asks. "If Juan is a hit, that is."

"Possibly," I say, looking over at Kenzie Perl. "But who knows? There could be more. Kenzie was pretty worried about the DJ station being stolen. And she's definitely the type to have items of value on her."

"True," Trissa says. "Do you think Kenzie might be a victim?"

I set my mouth in a grim line. "Maybe. Or she could be next."

11

TODAY, OUR LIFE SCIENCE TEACHER, Mr. Hicks, is
reading us a narrative nonfiction essay about Humphrey,
this whale that kept getting stuck after wandering into
San Francisco Bay. Not a lot of people know this about
me, but I *love* whales. I actually remember reading the
picture book account when I was in third grade. To me,
Humphrey was a lot like me: so curious that he had to
keep going no matter what.

But, today, I'm more than curious. I'm on a mission.

Juan Madrigal sits three seats in front of me and one
row over, so it won't be easy to talk in class. Maybe if we
split up into groups . . .

I raise my Lita pen and twirl it impatiently.
Unfortunately, Mr. Hicks takes this as a raised hand and
calls on me with a huge smile.

"Drew! Do you have something to add?"

I flush red. "Um, no. Sorry, Mr. Hicks."

He looks a little disappointed, but continues with the lecture. Which . . . am I even *listening* to the lecture? Isn't part of the Plan to get top-tier grades so that I get into the FBI?

Nervously, I open my school planner. I've been so immersed in Mom and the mystery for the last few days that I realize I'm not sure if I have anything due today. I wasn't exactly the best student yesterday, obsessing over my notes and the coffee date with Mom. I let out a sigh of relief when I see that everything is checked off.

"Let's break off into pairs to label the parts of humpback, orca, and blue whales," Mr. Hicks instructs.

I don't waste any time. Darting forward, I sidle up next to Juan. "Can I be your partner?" I ask.

He looks surprised, probably because this is the first time I've talked to him unprovoked. "Um, sure."

Juan is one of those seventh graders who often gets mistaken for a teacher even though he's barely thirteen. He's tall and broad-shouldered, with light brown skin and the hint of a mustache already forming above his lip. It's only when you look at his face that you see the shy seventh grader he really is. Maybe Juan is a little like Humphrey—a gentle giant.

He's also really smart. I know based on my observations (awards for academic achievement in sixth *and* seventh grade) but also on the fact that he's labeling whale parts like he's in a race right now. Trissa would tell me to ease in more slowly, but I have a feeling I'll need to be direct to distract him from the work.

As I start to label the humpback whale, scrawling *Median notch*, followed by *Dorsal ridge*, I look up at Juan. "So, Juan. I heard you might be missing a watch."

When I mention the watch, he stops writing and looks up in surprise. "How did you know that?"

"My phone got stolen," I say, keeping up my ruse from earlier. "From the PE lockers. And I thought I heard you say your watch went missing."

Juan looks like he might cry. "Yeah, mine was stolen from my PE locker too," he says. "My *abuelo*'s watch. He got it in Spain, like, sixty years ago."

So, Juan's theft was from the PE lockers too! I resist the urge to scribble exclamation points in my notebook.

"Is it a special brand, or very expensive?" I ask.

Juan shakes his head. "I don't know. I mean, it's nice-looking. I think the watch brand was Tiso? Tissot? It looked French or something. But, it's not like I need a watch. I only started wearing it after he died last year."

"I'm really sorry," I tell him, feeling a stab of guilt for bringing it up. "Can I ask, was anything else left behind?"

Juan gives me a funny look. "Actually, yeah. My allowance money. Only ten bucks, but still. It was weird. Like, who wouldn't take cash if you were stealing? Also, I have no idea how they got in. I *always* lock my locker. Since the watch is loose, I take it off for PE and I'm really careful about it—" He breaks off. "Not careful enough, I guess."

It really is strange, I think after we finish and I migrate back to my seat. Only Zora wasn't sure if she used a lock. And nobody had reported a broken or smashed lock. How is the thief getting in?

When I get to the library at lunchtime, only Trissa is waiting for me.

I furrow my brow. "Where's Shrey? I thought we were supposed to meet up here before we question Aiden Rullhausen."

Trissa smirks. "You didn't see his text?"

"No," I mutter, reaching into my bag to retrieve my phone. Usually, I'm more covert about hiding my phone when I'm using it, since the rule is "No phones, from bell to bell." But the library rules are more relaxed. Mr.

Covacha usually ignores phone use if it's not disruptive.

When I open my phone, I see the text:

Jedi Detective Agency MMS; Me, Trissa Jacobs, and 1 other

> **SHREY:** Can I skip this one? I need to emotionally prepare.

The text is followed by a GIF of a meditating cartoon unicorn.

"Emotionally prepare for questioning *Aiden*?" I wonder out loud.

"Umm, I'm thinking he has to prepare for asking Zora to the dance," Trissa suggests.

"Ohh," I murmur. "*Oh*. You think he's going to ask her today? Like, officially?"

"Well, it is Friday," she says. "If he doesn't do it today, he'd have to call her over the weekend. Right?"

"Yeah. I guess," I say.

Uh-oh. The twinge is back, and it does *not* feel good.

Am I jealous, though? Every time it comes up that Shrey likes Zora, or that she likes him—it's not like I get upset about *that*. It's just easier to think of Shrey's crush on Zora as this whole separate entity. Like, if my life was a timeline, them getting together should just naturally flow into that line seamlessly.

I think what's really bothering me is the idea of Shrey and Zora off on their own. Like, *without* me and Trissa.

"But . . . we're happy for Shrey, right?" Trissa asks. "I'm totally Team Zorey."

"I thought we landed on Shrora," I say.

Trissa sticks her tongue out. "No! That was literally the worst one. What about Scurhotra? Or Mallock?"

"Sorry," I say airily. "It's Shrora. The fates have spoken."

Trissa stares at me until I shift uncomfortably. "Are you jealous?" she asks.

"What?" I sputter.

"Sorry. I didn't mean for it to sound like that. It's just that you don't seem psyched about him asking her to the dance. Did you want him to take *you*?"

"Really? We're back on you asking if I like Shrey again?"

Trissa was fairly relentless in her questioning when we first became friends. I'm pretty sure she assumes that any time a boy and a girl hang out that much, it must *mean* something.

"No, I know you don't like him like that," Trissa assures me. "But maybe you wanted to go to the dance as a group or something?"

"I don't want to go at all," I tell her honestly. "Do *you* want to go as a group?"

"No!" Trissa says, but I notice a few things:

OBSERVATIONS:

- She covers her mouth when she says the word.
- She looks away from me and stares at the books to her left.

CONCLUSION: Trissa is *totally* lying to me right now.

"Yes, you do," I say.

"All right, fine!" she whispers. "I guess I kind of assumed we'd go as a group, and then it wouldn't be weird that I wasn't going *with* someone. It's too weird to go by myself. I mean . . . what? I'm supposed to third-wheel it with *Shrora*?"

At this, both of us break out into giggles.

"But, wait," I say. "What about Liz? You hang out with her."

"I do, but she's going with *her* group. She and I are

friends, but you and Shrey are *my* group. And you and Shrey fight. Like, all the time."

I wince. "Is that why you were upset the other night at my house?"

"You noticed that?" she asks in a small voice. "Yeah, kinda. That's one reason why I'm into the idea of having Zora and Alix as additions. More people would make us stronger. You know?"

I shake my head. Once again, the social norms of middle school are totally eluding me. I still don't get why Trissa couldn't hang out with Liz's group, or why a group needs a certain number of people to be strong. But then I remember how vulnerable Shrey and I were in grade school when it was only us. Maybe if we'd known Trissa then, it could have been different.

I take a breath and, before I can stop myself, say, "I guess we're going to the dance."

Trissa knocks me over with a hug. "Omigod, you're the *best*!" she yells.

"I don't particularly want to," I say with a laugh after she lets me go. "But you're my friend. And I want to know what they're going to do with a ten-foot yeti."

Trissa laughs. "Same."

"Can I ask you something, though?" When Trissa nods, I go on. "Is there someone you *would* have wanted to go with? Like a boy? It is boys you like, or so I've observed."

Trissa purses her lips. "There are a few boys I don't find disgusting."

My eyes widen visibly. "Like who?"

She looks around conspiratorially and shushes me. "Shhh. I can't say that here at school. Let's talk about it this weekend. We'll hang out to talk about the case, right?"

"I assume so," I say with a shrug. "It depends on how this talk with Aiden goes. The mystery could be solved in the next hour."

"Yeah. We should find him. Is he our top suspect at this point?" Trissa asks. "Oh, and how did the talk with Juan go?"

I quickly fill her in, confirming that Juan's theft fits the pattern. Then, I frown down at my notebook which has each suspect name written in spooky black ink:

Emma Cruz

Aiden Rullhausen

Alix Chang?

"It's really too bad about Emma. I *did* like her for it," Trissa says.

I grin at her. "Shrey would say you sound too much like me."

Trissa shrugs. "It was bound to happen."

We gather our bags and head for the front entrance. I cast a nervous glance at the clock on our way out: 12:50. We only have twenty minutes to find our top suspect and question him about the thefts. But in a rare (for me, anyway) stroke of good luck, we don't need to search. Trissa and I are barely outside the door before we see him, looking forlornly at the library.

"Um, hi, Aiden," I greet him.

"Hi," he says, his voice matching his expression.

"Are you . . . waiting to go inside the library?" Trissa asks carefully.

"I can't." He doesn't go on, but stares miserably at the entrance behind us.

"Does this have something to do with the book fair?" I ask gently. "Or the other things that have been getting stolen lately?"

Aiden immediately buries his face in his hands. When he comes up, his face is bright pink. "You know I did it, okay? Why don't you just *ask* me?!"

12

IN ONE OF DR. MIYAMOTO'S voice recordings on *Game Over*, she says that the best way to get a suspect talking is by *not* talking. People are motivated to fill silences—sometimes to the point of confession. So, when Aiden bursts out with this statement, I quickly eye Trissa and shake my head inconspicuously. She gets my meaning, and we both stay silent until he goes on.

"It's not fair!" he moans.

"What's not fair?" I ask, trying to leave as much of an opening as possible.

"I really wanted that book. Everyone was going around bragging about all the stuff they got at the fair. Water bottles, journals, UV pens, those scented gummy bear erasers," he lists off. "I couldn't even afford one book."

"You couldn't afford the book?" Trissa repeats gently. "I mean, that makes sense. It's one of the pricier books at the fair."

"How many books did *you* get?" he asks Trissa, a hint of accusation in his voice.

"Five," she admits. "Look, I know I'm lucky that my parents give me the money—"

"It's not about my parents giving me the money," he says with a humorless laugh. "They don't have the money. Almost nobody who lives in Cypress does. Or who lives below the freeway line. It's different than it is up here."

I lower my eyes, understanding his meaning. Ella Baker Middle School is in the foothills of Oakland, so it draws from what most residents call the "flats" as well as the hills. Like it is in most cities, the higher up in the hills you get, the richer the families get. Aiden must be from one of the three neighborhoods southwest of the freeway line that come up the hill to school.

I certainly don't feel rich. Since Mom left, it seems like we're scrimping even more than usual. But, then again, what did I say about the neighborhood Zora lives in, Clearview Heights? Wasn't I feeling a bit resentful of the kids who live up there because they clearly have more money than me? How could I blame Aiden for thinking the same thing about us?

Especially since I might have money coming my way, I think. For so long, Dad and I have had to budget to afford things. Is he getting any of that trust money that Mom mentioned? Am I being totally selfish by planning to use all of it for school when we had to bend over backward to justify our Netflix subscription last month? The thoughts churn, pushing in on each other, as I stare at Aiden.

It all seems like first-world problems in comparison to what he's going through. Here I am, obsessing about what to do with this money from Mom's family, when Aiden can't even afford a book. Looking at Trissa, I can tell she feels the same way.

He seems to sense our discomfort as he says, "Look, I'm sorry. It's not, like, *your* fault that you can afford books. I just wish I could. I love to read. And now I'm not even allowed in the library for two weeks." His face crumples, the pink shade deepening into a bright cherry red.

"It's not fair that you couldn't get a book," I say. "But next time you should ask Mr. Covacha. He's always complaining about all the junk kids get at the book fair when they should be getting books. I've seen him lend kids the money when they don't have it. He uses cash from the donation box, and sometimes he takes it from his own wallet."

Aiden looks up at me. "He does?"

I nod. "I worked at the fair this year. I saw a bunch of kids get a discount or a free book. Mr. Covacha says that getting books into kids' hands is the whole point of the fair. But you're going to have to apologize to him. And to all the other students who you stole from."

Aiden's expression runs through hopefulness to confusion. "What?" he says when I finish. "What students?"

"The things you stole from the PE lockers," Trissa fills in. "I mean, if you haven't sold them already. But it's going to be okay. If you make it right—"

"Whoa, whoa," Aiden says, putting his hands up. His cheeks are glistening and his eyes look between us wildly. "I stole the book. I admitted that. I already got in *trouble* for that. But I have no idea what you're talking about with the lockers. Other stuff was stolen?"

Trissa and I eye each other. Should we reveal anything about the locker thefts? It's possible that Aiden is lying. That being said, he admitted to stealing the book so openly, and he looks genuinely upset. Why would he lie now?

"Someone has been taking stuff from the lockers," I

explain. "A watch, a bracelet, some makeup, and a few other things. And whoever it is has been . . . leaving *notes*." I watch his face, unblinking, when I bring up the notes. Just in case it throws him off enough to confess.

"Why would I steal makeup?" he asks.

Trissa shrugs with her mouth. "I don't know. To sell, maybe? Some of the stolen things were pretty pricey."

"I wouldn't even know how to sell jewelry and makeup," he says, raising his hands pleadingly. "I swear. I only took the book."

He looks so upset to be accused that I rush to say, "Okay, okay. We believe you."

"But you should apologize to Mr. Covacha," Trissa urges him. "It'll be okay."

Aiden looks visibly relieved. "All right," he says. "I'll try."

Trissa and I say our goodbyes and head back into the library. We only have a little over ten minutes until the bell rings, but it's one of those strange warm January days that creeps up on the Bay Area every once in a while. Outside equals sweating through our T-shirts and jogger pants. Inside equals air-conditioning.

"Well, that was a bust," Trissa says as we walk through the doors.

"Lita would say that any suspect elimination is a

victory, as long as you have another lead to follow," I point out.

"Do we, though? Have another lead, I mean?"

I frown. "Meh. Not a solid one. But—"

I break off when I see someone I recognize behind the library counter. It's Sarina Masoumi, of the Kenzie Perl trio. I remember seeing her on the library volunteer list, but she didn't jump out at me as a suspect until now.

"Drew. What is it?" Trissa asks. "You look like you just saw a ghost."

"Does Zora know Sarina Masoumi?" I rush to ask.

Trissa shrugs. "I'm not sure. Why?"

I set my jaw. "Because she's slipping something into the library holds. Little pieces of paper. As in, possible *ransom* notes."

"Whoa. Do you think . . ."

"Yep. I think we may just have our next lead."

13

"SARINA!" I SAY, APPROACHING THE counter with Trissa behind me. "I didn't know you volunteered here at lunch."

Sarina looks both ways, like she's not sure if I'm talking to her. "Um, yeah. I started this semester. Just this week, though, because I was out and then I had a make-up test last Friday."

Hmmm. So that's why I didn't see her on book fair preview day.

"You're friends with Kenzie and Olivia, right?" Trissa asks. "Are you on the dance committee too?"

Once again, I smile gratefully at Trissa. For a newbie to the whole detective thing, she's awesome at putting people at ease. I might be great at profiling and observation, but when it comes to making people feel comfortable, I'm not a pro.

As soon as Trissa asks the question, Sarina's demeanor changes.

"Yeah!" she says. "I'm helping out after school today. Well, after yet another make-up test," she adds, rolling her eyes.

"That's a bummer. Why so many make-up tests?" I ask.

"I was out the first two weeks after winter break. Visiting my family in London," Sarina explains. Her tone is easy at first, but then she narrows her eyes at me. "Why?"

"Just curious." I try to keep my tone light as I slip behind the counter next to her.

"Umm," Sarina says, her voice rising.

"It's okay, I work here," I say with a laugh. "I'm just grabbing Trissa's holds."

Sarina frowns. "Okay, I guess."

Quickly, I scan the holds shelf. It actually looks like *every* book has an extra-bright blue piece of paper sticking out. I check for *Scurlock, Z* but it looks like Zora doesn't have any more holds today. I grab Trissa's two holds (because of *course* she has holds ready) and note that the paper is a tiny flyer. It's not a ransom note, but a slim bookmark-size sheet with festive font and a clip art disco ball. The text reads: *WONDERLAND DANCE—BE THERE!*

"Advertising?" I ask Sarina.

"Mr. Covacha told me I can put them in," Sarina replies with a shrug. "I'm on posters and flyers. It's kind of my job."

"All right, well, I guess I'll check these out now," Trissa says, handing the books to Sarina and exchanging a disappointed look with me.

"We'll see you later," I say to Sarina after she checks out Trissa's books.

"Drew!" a familiar voice cuts me off. I peer over toward the book fair and see Zora waving at me from the stacks.

"Is it my imagination or did Sarina glare at us for that whole conversation?" Trissa whispers as we walk over.

"Looked that way to me," I say with a shrug. "I've never exactly gotten a friendly vibe off her, but I don't think she's our thief."

"Because the papers were Wonderland dance flyers?" Trissa asks.

"And because, if she really was absent the first two weeks of this semester, there's no way she could have stolen from Jazz *or* Preethi."

"I'm so glad I tracked you down!" Zora exclaims as

soon as we sit down in our usual spot in the 800s section.

Trissa and I fill her in about eliminating Emma and Aiden. After I finish, I pause, thinking about how to frame a question I've been waiting to ask since Wednesday. "Zora, is it possible that someone close to you could have taken the bracelet? Even . . . a best friend?"

Zora's eyes pop. "Wait, like Alix? No way!"

"Sometimes people do strange things when they're angry. Have you two been in a fight? Or maybe if she thought you knew about the other thefts—"

"I'm telling you, no!" Zora insists. "Alix has the same bracelet. Why would she want to steal mine? That's just not her. We *never* fight. I promised myself after last year I would never be friends with someone who was all about the drama. Alix is, like, zero drama."

"It's really nothing personal," Trissa rushes to say. "If we're going to find your bracelet, we have to rule people out. And Drew saw Alix in your locker yesterday."

Zora's eyes fill with sudden understanding. "Oh! That's why you think it was her? Since I don't have PE Thursdays, she told me she'd check in case my bracelet was returned."

"That's what she said, too," Trissa says. "Sorry we had to ask."

"That's okay," Zora says. "I understand."

"What did you mean about Alix being zero drama?" I wonder. "Did something happen last year—something with more drama than you'd like?"

She blinks. "Oh, it's nothing. I was friends with these girls in sixth grade, but it was way too intense. They wanted me to dress like them, talk like them, and like everything they liked. It was creepy. And they were always turning on each other. One time, Olivia told me and Sarina to give Kenzie the silent treatment. I went along with it and it felt awful. I'm not like that." She shakes her head and cringes, as if she's reliving the incident.

"Sarina Masoumi?" I confirm, widening my eyes at Trissa, who returns the look.

"Yeah. Sarina, Olivia, and I were friends from Cesar Chavez, actually. But once you added Kenzie to the mix . . ."

"It got complicated?" Trissa guesses.

"You could say that. I mean, Olivia and Sarina were never that bad. But they started buying into the drama and, eventually, all three of them were horrible. It felt like . . . well, you know what a metamorphic rock is, right?"

"Sure," Trissa says. "It's a rock that changes because

of lava, or high pressure or something. Right?"

"Exactly. Well, every day with them felt like I was under this pressure to change. But I didn't want to change. I wanted to be me. And maybe 'me' is a nice limestone, or dolomite, or . . ."

Both of us grin from ear to ear at Zora, and she immediately trails off and looks away self-consciously.

"It's okay to be a nerd. We like nerds," Trissa says.

Zora laughs. "Okay, you asked for it. Because I have an actual book of geology jokes that I'll unleash on you. But I'll save that for later."

Intrigued as I am by the idea of a whole book full of geology jokes, I don't want to lead us too far off course.

"So, these girls wanted to change you into a carbon copy," I summarize. "Do you think any of them could be upset that you left the group and started hanging out with Alix?"

"I guess so. Them picking on Alix is the reason I left."

My ears perk up. "They picked on Alix? How so?"

Zora presses her lips into a thin line, as if retrieving the memory has already upset her. "Sarina made up this rumor that Alix was in love with Kenzie. She even bought a binder and wrote Alix's name on it. Then she put Kenzie's name in all these hearts. Olivia went along with it and, I don't know. It was like Sarina had totally changed into this other person. It was so messed up to use Alix as part of their fight, just because Alix likes girls."

Alix likes girls? I think to myself, wondering how I don't have any notes on that. Then again, I didn't notice Zora being a part of the Kenzie gang last year either. I take out my Lita pen and jot down a few notes.

"You know, Sarina *is* a volunteer at the library," I say. "Which means she has access to the library holds."

"You think Sarina stole my bracelet?" Zora asks, cringing.

"Well, the thing is, she has an alibi for the first two thefts," Trissa pipes in. "We were just about to add her to the suspect list, but she told us she was absent for the first two weeks of school. Unless she's not telling the truth . . ."

Zora cuts in. "Actually, I know that Sarina was in London for the first two weeks of school. Our moms are still friends. It was a big family reunion with her London family, and some family from Iran."

My face falls. Another lead out the window.

"Okay," I say. "Thanks, Zora."

The bell sounds, and suddenly—as though he's been creeping there the whole time—Shrey comes into view.

"Hey, Zora," he says, his voice wavering nervously.

"Hi, Shrey! Drew and Trissa were just filling me in on case updates." She looks up at him shyly, and moves a hand to brush her hair behind her shoulders.

"Um, that's great. Sooo . . . could I walk you to class? I wanted to talk to you about, uh, something?"

"Sure!" she says, her cheeks glowing as she follows Shrey out of the library.

Trissa gives me an amused look, but a strange feeling twisting in my gut prevents me from returning the gesture.

This is so weird. I like Zora. I *really* like her, actually. She's kind, and delightfully geeky. I even like the idea of her and Alix joining our group.

So, as he walks away from us, why does it feel like I'm losing my best friend?

14

BEING A KID, I KNOW I'm supposed to love weekends. Saturday and Sunday are when you're supposed to let loose, or relax. But for me? Nope. The weekend is nothing but an opportunity to fixate on all the bad things that happened during the week.

By Saturday, while Dad and I watch old episodes of *Forensic Files*, I'm officially obsessing. The whole weird twinge about Shrey, Zora, and the dance is sending me into a full spiral. Sure, I still don't want to kiss Shrey. Or hold his hand. But I can't say I'm not feeling jealous.

Basically, I'm a ginormous mess.

It's not like I never imagine kissing anyone these days. For a while, I thought I'd find the idea disgusting *forever*. Truthfully, the idea has been sliding into my mind like an uninvited guest. Although *never* with people I know, and definitely not Shrey.

I tend to have crushes on fictional characters, not actual people. It's easier that way. It doesn't really matter if they're boys or girls. I can have heart eyes for Rapunzel just as easily as for Flynn Rider. Truthfully, there are times I could almost imagine kissing them. But the person in my mind still isn't really me. It's an older, more put-together version of myself. A version that suddenly *likes* kissing, like when you grow up and suddenly like asparagus.

Dad is staring at me right now, his forehead making little worried creases. Which I guess I can't blame him for, since I'm barely watching *Forensic Files*.

"Are you still going to be okay with having Mom over for dinner?" he asks. "We could cancel if you need to."

"No, it's okay," I say. "But I might be done with *Forensic Files*."

Dad's jaw drops. "I've been watching hours of graphic murder reenactments and that's still the most disturbing thing I've ever heard."

Laughing, I say, "Not forever! I just have some work to do before Mom comes over."

He gives me a knowing look. "Are you crime-boarding again? Do we need to put on some Liszt? Maybe put in another order for red yarn?"

"Ha-ha," I retort. "I'm trying to figure out who would want to take Zora's bracelet."

"Who are your suspects?" he asks.

"Well, unfortunately, I eliminated all three of my top suspects this week," I grouse. "But I added a few more, since it sounds like Zora had a bad falling-out with a group of friends last year. Still, I feel like I need to make some more notes. I don't have evidence."

"How's my stocking stuffer holding up?" Dad asks. "For your notes, I mean."

"The Alchemist's Dungeon ink?" I ask. When he nods, I say, "Great. But I'm almost out. I actually might need to switch to ballpoint until I can make it over to the art store."

He gasps in mock horror. "That is a tragedy. Go ahead and take a twenty out of my wallet. It's on me."

"Best dad ever," I say, hugging him tightly.

Once I head to my room, I take out the crime board. Truthfully, I'm glad that Dad didn't press me too hard on the mystery, since it's way more than a missing bracelet at this point. I do feel guilty for not telling him about all the other thefts, though. After the Ella Baker Shade mystery, I promised to be honest with Dad.

On the other hand, I'm twelve years old. I'm being honest about Mom, about school, and about the fact that

I'm helping Zora find her bracelet. Don't I get to keep some things to myself?

That rationalization keeps my usual asthma flare-up and stomach cramping at bay, so I let it go. After checking some old notebooks and updating the information on Kenzie and Olivia, I tuck the crime board under my bed and head out to set the table. Then I put the Lita pen in my backpack, switching it out for an inferior, clicky-top pen until I can stock up on ink.

"Sweetheart!" Dad calls from the kitchen. "Can you bring out the food?"

I walk into the kitchen and dutifully pick up a large dish of ratatouille. "Mom's favorite," I point out. "Did you get French bread, too?"

"Even though French bread is an affront to my people, I did."

"An affront to your people . . . the Leclairs?" I joke. "Dad, you're literally French."

"French, *and* Bulgarian, *and* Lithuanian! Besides, I meant bakers. Everyone from my community knows that sourdough is superior."

Giggling at his antics, I walk the ratatouille into the dining room and set it down. Ten minutes later, Mom rings the doorbell.

"Sorry I'm late!" Mom explains airily. "The Lyft

driver said six minutes but it was more like fifteen. Oh! Ratatouille! You remembered." She looks at Dad fondly.

He smiles, but I can tell by the way the corners of his mouth stretch a bit too wide that the smile is forced. It makes me wonder if he's mad that she was a few minutes late, or if there's something else they're fighting about.

Mom sits down and places her napkin delicately on her legs. "How was the rest of your school week?" she asks me. "Anything . . . *new* with Shrey? You said he might have a date to that dance?"

Her tone is just awkward enough that I cast a sharp look at Dad. I didn't talk to her about the whole Shrey-trying-to-kiss-me thing since it happened after she decided to leave. Did he tell her about that? I bristle, imagining them talking about the kissing thing like it's a cute anecdote.

"Shrey asked Zora Scurlock to the Wonderland dance," I say.

"Oh!" Mom says. "Good for Shrey. I always thought he liked you, but I'm glad he found someone."

Dad gives her a sharp look, while I stare at the French bread on her plate, which she still hasn't taken a bite of. All she keeps doing is taking these tiny bites of tomato and eggplant. I don't know why, but it irritates me.

"Anyway, Trissa and I are going to the dance together,"

I go on nervously. "But with Shrey and Zora, and her friend Alix. It's sort of a *group* thing, I guess. Or that's what Trissa says."

"Trissa is a new friend of Shrey and Drew's," Dad explains.

"Girlfriend?" Mom asks.

I practically choke on my bread. "What? Um, no. We're friends. Like me and Shrey."

"Okay," she says mildly, finally grabbing a small piece of bread herself. Her words are casual enough, but they make me feel exposed. Can she, like, tell from looking at me that I like boys and girls?

It makes me wonder, what would it be like if Mom knew something deeper about me? Would it be like true crime, with her endlessly needling me about trying "other activities"? Or would she actually accept that it's who I am?

Part of me assumes she would think that it's just too much. *Drew*, I can masochistically picture her saying, *you're already so different from your other classmates. With all your illnesses, and your . . .* unique *extracurricular activities. Why add something else?*

But I have to admit that another part of me desperately hopes she'll just roll with it this time. That she'll accept at least this part of me for *me*.

I don't get the chance to force the issue, because the conversation naturally shifts away from the dance. Nothing goes wrong, exactly, but I find myself fixating on the idea of telling Mom, and imagining all the horrible ways that it could go. Then, I imagine all the ways I *could* react, but probably wouldn't. It sets my nerves on edge until I finally ask to be excused. When I collapse onto my bed, I instinctively reach for my earbuds and turn on *Game Over.*

When the Masterpiece Man ended up at the National Portrait Gallery in Washington, DC, he was in Dr. Miyamoto's backyard. After only a few weeks on the case, our good doctor didn't think it was a coincidence. She was closing in on him, but was he closing in on her, too?

Suddenly, I hear a familiar voice. A scratchy, somewhat faraway-sounding recording plays in one of Gerald and Max's interludes. It's Lita! She's reading aloud the letter she'd written to Masterpiece Man. The letter had never been sent, of course; it was more like a promise to herself that she'd catch him.

"You would never expect a woman to show up at your door, would you? To you, women and girls are just pieces of art—objects to be manipulated as part of your sick game. You don't believe a woman could be smart

142

enough to catch you. When I show up at your door, you'll never suspect that it's me who ended the game. But it will be me."

"It will be me." I say my new personal refrain aloud.

I hadn't ever *heard* the letter like that. It had been published as part of an interview in the *New York Times*, but actually listening to it gives me goosebumps. Lita said that she had written it when her favorite suspect turned out to have an alibi. Everything had been pointing to this one person, but suddenly, all the leads went cold and she had to start from scratch. *Maybe if I use my Lita pen to write a letter to the thief, it will motivate me. I still have a little ink left . . .*

The sound of raised voices distracts me before I can grab my pen. Mom and Dad. *Again*. Their voices are too low to hear, so I quietly open the door and slip into my usual position on the hallway floor.

"I don't know why it's so wrong that I ask about my daughter's life," Mom is saying tearily. "I don't *know* anything. I didn't even know you visited my mother until *she* called me."

"I told you about the situation with Shrey and Drew in confidence," he says evenly. "I wanted you to have all the information after she left you that message."

I flinch, feeling suddenly hot. He's clearly talking

about the message I left Mom last fall—the one where I told her to stay away forever. I know Dad probably tells her a lot because of the coparenting thing, but the idea of him sharing the Shrey stuff makes me flush with humiliation.

"Did you even know about this dance?" she accuses. "These things are important to girls her age."

"Maybe to girls like you, but not to *Drew*," Dad says.

"But she's going," Mom counters. "Maybe those teen hormones are coming. Are you even ready for that, Sam?"

I can practically hear him rubbing his temples in frustration. "I'm perfectly ready for that, Jenn. But Drew has told me that romantic relationships don't interest her now."

"Maybe she's not being as open with you as you think," I hear Mom retort. "Do you even know this Trissa person? Could she be starting to have an interest in girls?"

"If she is, who cares?" Dad explodes. "Trissa happens to be a friend, but what difference does it make if she ends up liking boys or girls?"

I wince, bracing myself for Dad to tell her about the conversation we had about crushes on both boy and girl characters on TV, but he doesn't.

"Don't do that. Don't make it out like I'd be upset if Drew was gay. You *know* I only care that she's happy. It's just that she was bullied for so long. I only worry about her getting bullied for this, too. I don't want her to have to go through that again."

"You're not exactly around enough to know what she's going through, Jenn."

I can't help but want to cheer for Dad at that moment. It's true. Mom keeps talking about dances and hormones. Does she wish they would turn me into the "normal" daughter of her dreams? Like, do girls get their periods and suddenly leave behind everything they like? Is she hoping that those hormones she talked about will suddenly make me realize that mysteries are—what did she call it?

A childish *fantasy*.

Well, sorry, Mom. I got my period over winter break, and guess what? I still really want to read about catching serial killers.

"I may not be here every second but I know my own daughter," Mom hits back after a moment. Her voice sounds heavy, like she might be crying. "Is this about me and Dustin?"

"No, it's not about you and Dustin. It's about you and Drew. It's about where you live now," Dad counters.

"*This* is something she's going through."

"God, Sam, I'm so tired of you on your high horse! It's not like I'm the only one who's moving on. What about your little girlfriend?"

Wait, *what*?!

"Jenn . . ."

"No, really. Have you even told Drew about—"

"*Stop*," he says in a quiet but furious voice. "Let's talk outside."

I hear the back patio door slide open and closed, and the sounds of their voices fade into distant tones I can't understand.

Little *girlfriend*?

So, I was right. That must be what Dad said he wasn't ready to talk about the other day. Still, overhearing it like that . . . it felt awful. Dad and I are supposed to be a team. Right? Why would he tell Mom and not me?

And why are they still fighting about me all the time? Am I still this huge problem, like a big, socially awkward rock standing between them? I mean, I know they're getting divorced. I've been preparing for divorce. But will they ever even get through a dinner without yelling?

I'm starting to get legit upset now, so I use my tried-and-true method to help me calm down. Basically, it's making note of everything in the room around me until I land on something that distracts me. My vision blurs with tears of exhaustion and bewilderment but, finally, my eyes rest on the partially obscured crime board by my bed. The red string sags between tacked-up items, half of which have been crossed out or switched up.

Now, it looks like I have *two* mysteries to solve. Three, if you count the strange feeling I'm having about Shrey and Zora.

And, between all three, I don't have nearly enough leads.

15

SMS; Me, Jennifer Leclair

JENNIFER LECLAIR: Hi, honey! What about a
spa day at the Clearview, my treat?

I'LL BE HONEST. SPA DAYS aren't really my thing. I'm
way more of a stay-home-working-on-my-crime-board
type of person. That being said, the "Dad + Girlfriend"
reveal from the night before is totally weirding me out.
The healthy thing to do, of course, would be to talk to
him. But, why do that when I can subtly pump Mom for
clues over cucumber water and facials?

That's how, at ten the next morning, I find myself
wandering around the fanciest hotel I've ever seen. So

fancy that I consider checking the restaurant menu to see if they have those gourmet tater tots Trissa had mentioned.

The Clearview Hotel is one of the oldest buildings in Oakland—a sprawling lodge with crisscrossing wooden beams and stained-glass windows. Every room looks like you could use the word *grand* to describe it. Even my mom's room has vaulted ceilings. It's almost like Disneyland, but instead of rides, there are miles of clean, white linens.

"I can't get over how grown-up you look!" Mom says when she sees me approaching the spa hostess station. She waves one hand up and down. "That outfit is so cute!"

I try to suppress a devious grin. That's what I'd been going for. I'd left behind my usual podcast tee and leggings in favor of a nice blouse that Grandma Joy bought me for my last birthday. It's so Mom's type, in fact, that I'm pretty sure it will distract her into falling right into my *very* specific line of questioning.

"The changing rooms are this way," the hostess tells us. She blinks at the large backpack I have slung over my shoulder. "You can leave . . . that in the personal items area."

I frown. I hate being away from my backpack for too long, in case I need to take notes. But I guess I can't actually take notes *while* I'm interrogating Mom.

We're ushered toward the changing rooms, where I get into a big white robe that looks softer than it is. By the time I come out, Mom is lounging in the waiting area, sipping her water.

"Cucumber water?" I ask.

"It's actually a house-made agua fresca with cucumber, grapes, and berries," Mom clarifies.

I pick up a glass and take a sip. "Holy refreshment!" I sputter.

Mom laughs. "I nearly forgot how funny you are," she says. "It's twenty-four-seven entertainment."

I flush, surprised to feel a warm glow of pride at the remark.

"That's me," I say. "Future criminal profiler and comedian."

She giggles again. "Hey! Speaking of which, how is that mystery at school coming?"

Practically spitting out my agua fresca, I stare at her. "Um, I thought you weren't so excited about that," I say carefully.

She lowers her eyes. "I know. I'm sorry. The truth is, I didn't see how it was all connected: these cases, and what you want to do when you're older. But, after we talked over coffee the other day, I realized that the mysteries are part of it. You know, the whole package. *Drew.*"

It's all I can do not to sputter in reply. Is this for real? Part of me feels suspicious. Mom has never taken an interest in what I'm actually interested in. But, maybe everything Dad has told her is finally sinking in. Is that even possible?

"Well, Shrey's new girlfriend had something stolen from her locker." I say the words slowly and deliberately, worried at each step that she'll throw her head back and laugh at me. Against all odds, she doesn't.

"Intriguing!" she says, sipping her water and not even sounding sarcastic. "How does she know it was stolen?"

I fill her in on a few of the more basic points of the case, making sure not to reveal more than what I've already told Dad.

"It sounds like one of you and your father's crime shows!" she says. "You two were always so alike."

The mention of Dad makes me realize that I've totally been talked into a corner and away from my mission to interrogate her about the mystery girlfriend.

Yikes. First Alix, now Mom. Am I off my game?

I glance at the clock over the archway and then back at Mom, who's already putting cucumbers on her eyes and leaning back. It's now or never. I mentally review

Lita Miyamoto's top three interrogation techniques.

OPTION 1: THINK FAST

If you cut the small talk and surprise them by asking point-blank questions, they might be taken aback enough to give an honest answer.

OPTION 2: THE OMNISCIENT INTERROGATOR

By pretending you already know what you *want* to know, the subject may feel comfortable or caught off guard enough to fill in the blanks.

OPTION 3: THE SYMPATHETIC EAR

The profiler uses all of their knowledge about the subject to try to form a bond with them, making them feel like they're not alone.

Based on all my observations of Mom, I think option

number two is my best bet.

"So, it's kind of weird, right?" I say. "Dad having a new girlfriend, I mean."

Mom peels one cucumber off her eye and regards me with astonishment. "He told you?"

I prop myself up on one elbow, facing her. "You know Dad. He tells me everything. But, you know . . . a *girlfriend*. I guess I didn't think it would happen this quickly."

"Well, I don't think it's too serious," Mom says with an air of knowledge. "They haven't even gone on a date yet."

"That's interesting," I say with a shrug. "I thought they had."

"What?" Mom asks sharply. She takes both cucumbers off of her eyes and looks at me. "He told me the opposite."

I'm starting to get the sense that my charade is going a bit too far, so I rush to dial it back. "I really have no idea. You're probably right."

"Okay," she says, leaning back and letting out a breath.

"You look relieved," I point out, unable to stop myself. "Why?"

She blinks. "Oh! No, sweetie, it's not that. I don't

mind who your father sees. I only expect that he would keep me in the loop, that's all."

Don't say it, Leclair. You and Mom are actually getting along and she's even asking about the crime stuff. Keep your mouth shut . . .

Nope. I can't not say it.

"Well, you didn't keep us in the loop. You know. With *Dustin.*"

Mom sucks in a long breath, and I think she's about to let me have it. But, after a few seconds, she says, "You're absolutely right."

"Wait, what?"

"You're right," she repeats. "Your father has every right to keep this to himself until Luna actually becomes a part of our lives."

Ah. Her name is *Luna.* But . . . who the heck is Luna?

"Jennifer and guest?" A serene voice breaks into my thoughts. "We're ready for you."

"Let's go!" I say, trying to create the perfect tone that says: *This is a light conversation! I definitely wasn't tricking you into revealing any secrets!*

"My treatment will be longer," Mom tells me. "Just leave your stuff here and enjoy the pool bar. I'll take care of the bill and meet you out there."

The facial itself isn't so bad. Bordering on good, even.

It's mostly a series of gentle washes, with a nice cool gel toward the end. I could get used to this. Maybe when Mom comes back here to visit, I'll convince her to get a room here again.

That's if *she visits again*, a little mean voice in my head says.

But, she will, right? She'd said that spending time with me was literally why she was here, hadn't she?

When I get cleaned up and walk out to the waiting area, the hostess says, "You can find drinks and snacks that way." She gestures toward an ornate wooden bar at the far end of the pool.

"Thanks." I walk over and review the menu while a cheerful-looking woman smiles at me from behind the register. "Can I get an orange dreamsicle smoothie?" After I tell the woman to charge it to Mom's room, a somewhat-familiar voice breaks the silence.

"She did *not!*" the voice protests.

"She did!" another voice confirms.

Sitting on a nearby cluster of cushioned patio chairs are none other than Olivia Campos, Kenzie Perl, and Sarina Masoumi.

Well, well, well. If it isn't two of my newest suspects.

Quickly ducking behind a large wooden column, I peer at the trio:

OBSERVATIONS:

• Kenzie wears expensive-looking sunglasses with an insignia that reads: *D&G*.

• Olivia has a fancy-*looking* swimsuit, but it's one I recognize from Target.

• Sarina fidgets with a colorful bracelet on her wrist while she listens to her friends, not partaking in the gossip quite as enthusiastically as the other two.

CONCLUSIONS: Kenzie can afford any of the stolen items. Olivia might have sent the ransom note to get more money to keep up with her friends' lifestyle. Not sure on Sarina, although her body language shows that she might be getting tired of Kenzie and Olivia like Zora did.

"Emma Cruz is *such* a—"

I make a little O with my mouth when I hear the word Kenzie uses. I don't disagree in theory but—*yeesh*.

"She didn't only break the yeti's arm," Kenzie is saying. "She completely messed up the decorations.

They're way too basic. We're going for a fun, nostalgic *wonderland*. Not some cheap, Walmart snow-globe scene."

"Yeah, and, um, she doesn't even care that your dad paid for everything," Sarina puts in.

"She doesn't. And her family certainly isn't chipping in," Kenzie replies with an eye-roll. "Not surprising, based on where she lives. She's a hiker, not a roller."

Olivia joins in when the girls laugh, but looks uncomfortable. I can't help but feel bad for her. Doesn't Kenzie know that she lives down the hill too, in Cypress? And how is Olivia affording this? Biting my lip, I start calculating what this spa day must have cost Mom. But she has money. Olivia doesn't seem to. Is Kenzie footing the bill?

I creep forward to see if I can hear better, but the conversation seems to have shifted.

"Do you like this color?" Sarina is saying, stretching her fingers out to show her manicure. "Or is it too orangey? It's orangey, isn't it?"

Kenzie tips her glasses down. "Hate to say it, but yeah. Orangey."

Olivia nods. "Definitely. But I can paint over it. I watched a ton of YouTube videos on how to get a straight polish by starting in the middle, and—"

"Drew!" a voice shouts at epic volume. "Order up for DREW?"

That was . . . less than inconspicuous. Trying to look relaxed, I stroll toward the counter to grab my order. When I turn back, all three girls are staring right at me.

"Hey. I know you," Olivia Campos says. For a second, I think she's eyeing me suspiciously. But, based on the knowing looks they trade, I realize that they're placing me as "that creepy girl who draws skulls." Or possibly "that girl whose mom ran away with the guidance counselor." I couldn't be so lucky as to hope that they're thinking of me as "the brilliant detective who took down the school's most notorious cyberbully."

"Drew," I remind them.

"What are you doing here?" Kenzie asks bluntly.

"My mom got us a spa treatment," I say, shifting uncomfortably. With us off campus, in puffy white robes, it doesn't feel like a prime interrogation moment.

A girl's gotta try, though. I think up a conversation starter, hoping it sounds natural.

"So, I heard you're all on the dance committee. How's that coming?" I try to act nonchalant as I take a long sip of my smoothie.

"Well," Kenzie says, leaning forward. "You probably heard us talking about Emma. But you're not going to tell her anything about that, right?"

"Why would I?" I ask.

Olivia gives me a look. "Um, because you're a narc. As in, you narc on people."

I slurp my smoothie. "You mean, a criminal informant for the narcotics department?"

"A what?" Olivia asks, giggling.

"That's literally what a narc is," I say.

"Whatever," Kenzie cuts in. "It's not like we care if Emma knows we hate her."

Olivia lets out a laugh. "That's true. After all, we have the power to make her life very difficult if she tries anything with us."

"Drew!" I hear another voice call, from behind me. It's Mom.

"Well, as interesting as this has been, I have to run," I say. "See you in school."

"*Sure*," Olivia says. That word alone causes all three of them to erupt into a giggle fit. It's definitely laughter at my expense, but I try to ignore that and focus on what they said as I walk away from the snack bar.

What did Olivia mean about the girls having the "power" to make Emma's life difficult? And how does any of this connect with the thefts?

"Were those your friends?" Mom asks as she walks up.

"Nope. Suspects."

Mom lowers her glasses. "Really? That's strange."

"Why?" I ask.

"Well, I know I'm not exactly an expert in this mystery stuff," she says. "But why would girls who can afford to come to the Clearview need to steal?"

I look at Mom with a smile. She may not be a true-crime person, like she said, but she's not wrong on that count.

Come tomorrow, I have some serious investigating to do.

16

IT'S ONLY AN HOUR INTO Monday morning, and I already wish I'd stayed in bed. Ever since the moment I woke up, things have been going wrong. Nothing major, but enough tiny things to make me feel like crawling under a rock.

Then, before school, Shrey doesn't show up to question our suspect. *Again.*

"Where is he?" I ask Trissa through gritted teeth when I find her sitting alone on the small bench next to the library garden.

"Probably with Zora," Trissa replies. "Since they're going to the dance together and have apparently been talking on the phone and texting *all* weekend."

I only nod tersely in reply. Shrey had also been texting me last night about every little thing Zora said.

"Everything okay?" Trissa asks. "We can go question Kenzie without him."

"I know," I say, softening my tone. "I'm sorry I'm so grumpy. I can't find my pen."

"The *Lita* pen?" Trissa asks, horrified.

"Yeah." I smile weakly at Trissa. That was truly the worst thing to have happened all day, I'll be honest. It's not exactly unusual for me to lose track of things. Dad likes to call my backpack "the black hole" because I lose so many things in there. But I was sure I'd packed it in the interior pocket until I could get more ink for it. Maybe it fell through the hole that's been forming in the lining?

"That's awful!" Trissa says, her forehead creasing with concern. "No wonder you're grumpy. Is anything else going on?"

"My mom wants to take me shopping. She and I have been getting along really well, but shopping has never worked out well for us. I think she wants me to pick out some kind of regular-girl-energy dress for the dance."

Trissa rolls her eyes. "She kind of *aggressively* doesn't get you."

"Eh. She's not so bad these days," I say, realizing that I mean it.

"That's true," Trissa says.

"At least she did this whole trip out to see me. Ah, I'm probably just complaining about nothing." I smile at her, some of my early-morning grump dissipating. Getting that off my chest really did make me feel lighter. So much so that, when Trissa gestures toward the path and says, "Shall we?" I reply, "Why yes, madam!" with comical formality. The two of us end up exchanging Edwardian-type phrases and giggling halfway to the multipurpose room.

When we get there, nearly everything is decorated. A giant banner that reads *Ella Baker in WONDERLAND!* stretches across the stage area. Giant white honeycomb puffs dangle like snowballs from the ceiling amid glimmering blue streamers, and they've added a giant sparkling disco ball in the center. I don't see the yeti, but I guess all the floor decorations are being stored until the night of the dance.

We spot Kenzie right away. It looks like she's supervising Olivia, who is hanging a winter-themed border around the stage by herself.

"Kenzie," I say as we walk up. "Can we talk to you?"

She looks between Trissa and me. "Why?"

For a moment, I panic. That's what I was supposed to do this morning. Come up with a good excuse to talk to Kenzie. I'm getting ready to wing it, but Trissa rescues me.

"It's about Emma," she says with an air of mystery. "Emma Cruz."

Kenzie's eyes flash with interest.

I may not be a hugger but, at this moment, it's difficult not to throw my arms around her. It's the perfect tease, after the conversation at the spa.

Olivia moves to follow us, but Kenzie cuts her off at the pass. "We need to finish that border," she says pointedly. Olivia opens her mouth to protest but merely glares after us, muttering as she turns her attention back to the border.

"What?" Kenzie snaps once we've got her alone.

"So, you may have seen me talking to Emma last week," I say. "She's not exactly a friend, but we are helping her with something."

"And?" Kenzie asks pointedly. "What does this have to do with me?"

"Someone stole her purse," Trissa puts in, starting to look annoyed. "The Swoon and Swank bag. And that's not the only one. Our friend Zora had a bracelet stolen, and two other girls have had things taken."

For a second, Kenzie almost looks nervous. Quickly, her eyes flit back to Olivia. It's only half a second, but definitely noticeable.

"Yeah, and?"

"And we were wondering if you've had anything stolen," I say carefully.

"Why would you think that?" Kenzie asks.

"Because you wear brand-name stuff a lot and that's what the thief is targeting," Trissa says, clearly noting my change in direction.

She blinks with relief. "Oh! I guess that makes sense. My dad has been *very* generous since SETEC went fiber-optic. But, no, I haven't had anything stolen."

"Great," I say. Before I go on, I meditate on the voice clip I'd heard on *Game Over*. Over the weekend. It was Lita, talking about her process in questioning a security guard at the National Portrait Gallery when she was closing in on Masterpiece Man.

"When questioning a witness who may be a suspect, I will occasionally add a crime that never happened at all. If the person is a valid suspect, they may tell you without telling you at all. The eyes are the window to the soul, but also to a possible lie."

"You know," I say, "a lot of the thefts were from the PE locker but I actually had my phone stolen in the library. Have you noticed anyone following you, either in the locker area or the library?"

Kenzie blinks with confusion. "The library? Why would I go to the library?"

Trissa's jaw drops. "Um . . . for books."

"Why? My parents buy me anything I want to read. We have a whole library room."

Trissa looks like she's not sure how to speak after that statement, which I get. I kind of want to kick Kenzie in her name-brand shoes right now.

"Look, I don't go to the library, and no one has been, like, stalking me in the locker room." Kenzie crosses her arms, and I take the hint that she's done talking.

"Okay, Kenzie. Thanks for your help."

The moment we set foot outside the library, Trissa shudders. "She doesn't *go* to the library? Like, ever? Who is this demon?"

"I know," I say. "It's hard to wrap my brain around. But, if she's not lying, I think that crosses her off the suspect list. She couldn't have left Zora's notes if she literally never goes to the library."

"But Kenzie did look weird when we started talking to her, right?"

"Definitely. But did you notice she looked over at Olivia?" I ask.

Trisssa's eyes widen. "No! I missed that."

The bell rings, and I wave to Trissa. "I'll ask Mr. Covacha about the library alibi during my TA period. See you at lunch? Hopefully with Shrey, if he still exists?"

She laughs. "See you then."

The first few periods drag on, but I manage to use the time to add to my working profile:

OFFENDER PROFILE

NAME: Unknown (Ella Baker Middle School's locker thief)

AGE: Likely 12–13

KNOWN VICTIMS: Jazz Aguilar, Juan Madrigal, Liz Davis, Preethi Agarwal, Zora Scurlock, Emma Cruz

MODUS OPERANDI: Steals items of value from the PE lockers.

SIGNATURE: Steals an item of value, but leaves money and other valuables behind.

POSSIBLE PERPETRATORS:

1) ~~Emma Cruz~~

2) ~~Aiden Rullhausen~~

3) ~~Alix Chang~~

4) ~~Sarina Masoumi~~

5) Olivia Campos

6) Kenzie Perl (maybe eliminated, confirm alibi)

ITEMS STOLEN:

1) Jazz—Suede jacket

2) Juan—Tissot watch

3) Liz—Harper Berry makeup palette

4) Preethi—Limited-edition iPhone case

5) Zora—Charm bracelet with garnet in a silver heart (inscribed?)

6) Emma—Swoon & Swank backpack purse

STATUS: At large.

By the time I get to the library, I've half convinced myself that Kenzie was lying about never going to the library. When I ask Mr. Covacha, however, he reacts right away.

"Kenzie Perl?" he says with an uncharacteristic edge to his tone. "That girl has only set foot in the library twice this year. Once for textbook check-out, and once for the library tour. Both were last August."

"So, you never see her here?"

He shakes his head. "Never ever. When I talked to her mom at Back-to-School night, she told me they *buy* her every book she wants and she has her own laptop and phone." Mr. Covacha shakes his head. "As if those are the only things you can do at the library."

"She's missing out," I say encouragingly.

"Thanks, Drew," Mr. Covacha says gratefully. Then, he snaps his fingers. "Drew!"

"Yes?"

He reaches into his back pocket and pulls out an

envelope, with my name written in big block letters. "I found this on the counter this morning. Not sure who left it."

The hairs on my arm stand at attention as goosebumps flush over the skin. A *letter*?

"Um, I'm just going to put my stuff away," I say, retreating into the back office. When I rip open the envelope and look at the paper inside, my heart sinks.

MISSING ANYTHING TODAY? BACK OFF, DREW LECLAIR. THIS IS YOUR ONE AND ONLY WARNING.

I fumble with the zipper on my backpack. Once again, my fingers don't find the Lita pen. Oh, no . . . is this the warning? It *has* to be.

I know I'm kind of a slob, but I treat the Lita pen like it's my baby. I put it in the same pocket of my backpack every day, and the pocket has a zipper so it doesn't fall out. After this note, there's no question. The thief stole the Lita pen as a threat.

My mind races back to the spa day. Even if Kenzie isn't our thief, *Olivia* might have seen me there earlier and gone through my backpack. It was in an open area. If Olivia had been watching me, she could have easily snatched the pen. Isn't that what the thief had said in the note to Zora? They were *watching* her.

I shove the letter into my sweats pocket and slip out of the office, relieved to find that Mr. Covacha is in the stacks. Quickly, I scan the holds shelf until I find what I'm looking for: a new hold filed under *Scurlock, Z.*

Swallowing hard, I flip through the pages. It's only a split second before the paper falls out. Another ransom note for Zora.

YOU NARCED ABOUT THE BRACELET AND NOW IT'S $100. AT THE DANCE TOMORROW, LEAVE THE MONEY IN THE GIRLS' BATHROOM. THE FOURTH STALL WILL BE OUT OF ORDER. LEAVE IT IN THE TAMPON BOX BY 7 PM. COME ALONE.

Narced.

Isn't that exactly the language Olivia used with me at the spa?

You narc on people.

Olivia, who was desperate to keep up with her friends' brand-name fashion. Who was friends with Zora before she bailed to hang out with Alix full time?

Olivia Campos is our thief. I'm *sure* of it.

17

Jedi Detective Agency MMS; Me, Trissa Jacobs, and 1 other

> **ME:** Meet in the 800s at lunch. Bring Zora and Alix. 911!

I'M NOT SURE WHAT I EXPECTED.

A little sympathy, possibly? A shocked expression? A promise that my *best friend* will do whatever it takes to help me find who took my prized possession?

At least Zora, Alix, and Trissa react appropriately. After I explain the meaning behind the pen, Zora looks horrified, and Alix rests a comforting hand on my shoulder. Trissa is the most shocked of all, actually throwing a hand to her chest and gasping.

"Not the Lita pen!" she cries.

They all get it. To me, that pen is special—like Zora's bracelet.

Shrey, however, isn't acting like I lost anything.

"The thief doesn't even say that they took the pen, though," he says, looking down at the note incredulously. "Are you sure you didn't lose it?"

If looks could kill, I would literally be murdering Shrey right now.

"I didn't lose it," I snap, grabbing the note back. "Trust me. Besides, what else could 'missing anything' mean?"

"I wasn't saying you *definitely* lost it. I'm just saying you tend to lose things. And that sometimes you end up suspecting the mailman or something. It's not like it never happens," he says.

"Thank you for that very accurate profile of Drew Leclair," I say sarcastically. "Maybe you should join me at Quantico."

"I guess I'm just not sure how she would know about the pen to take it," Shrey goes on. "Did you check your backpack to see if anything else is missing? I mean, not that you would know right away because your backpack is—"

"Shrey, don't *even*," I snap.

Trissa looks uneasily between us, her voice wavering as she says, "Come on, guys . . ."

Sensing her discomfort, and seeing the awkward look that Zora and Alix are trading, I decide to let it go. For now.

"Either way," I say pointedly, "we've got two more notes. And Olivia wrote them. I'm *sure* of it."

"Olivia," Zora repeats, toying with the ends of her tight curls. "But . . . we were friends."

"That means she's got a connection to you, which explains why you're the one she started sending notes to," Alix points out.

I blink at her, surprised. "Alix is one hundred percent right. Also, Olivia might have a reason to resent kids with money."

"That makes sense," Trissa says.

Zora shifts uncomfortably. "Yeah, I get it," she mumbles.

"We didn't mean you, Zora," Trissa rushes to add.

Zora reassures her, "It's just that I don't really think of myself that way. My parents aren't really spenders, like Kenzie and Sarina's families are."

"I know what you mean," I reply, thinking about what Mom told me about the trust for college. I bite my lip guiltily. "Look, it may not make a difference to us. But for someone else, it could be everything. Which could equal motive. The only problem with that theory is that kids from Clearview Heights aren't the primary targets. She's going after kids who don't necessarily have the money to replace the things she stole."

"There's one more problem," Alix says. "You're saying that Olivia doesn't live like Kenzie or Sarina, but she has to fit into this group that goes to the spa every other weekend. Also, she's . . . y'know. The *worst*. But if that's all true, wouldn't we be seeing all of the items for sale?"

I furrow my brow. "That is weird. Trissa looked into it, but nothing turned up. Maybe she's selling them to other students?"

"Maybe," Alix said. "I'm only wondering why Olivia would be leaving actual *cash* behind if it's about the money. And if cash isn't important, why send a ransom note to Zora? Something doesn't feel quite right."

"Maybe it's because this case is getting kinda creepy," Trissa points out. "Liz was totally freaked when it looked like someone just trashed her locker. Something being stolen is bad enough, but having someone go through your locker is super weird. People are scared to bring their stuff to school now, since locks aren't working."

"Even Emma seemed spooked," I agree. "I get it. The idea of someone going into my backpack makes me really uneasy. Maybe money isn't the motive. Everyone is scared, like you said. Maybe that's what Olivia wants."

"*If* someone went through your backpack," Shrey says, ignoring the epic side-eye that follows. "So, is Olivia really our only possible suspect? What about Jazz, or Preethi?"

"Why Preethi?" I ask. "Because she hates you?"

"Hey!" he protests.

Shrugging, I say, "She does, though."

"Fine. But remember last time we didn't know that Ella Baker Shade was Ethan because he was a victim of the posts."

"That's fair," I say, frowning. "We didn't really look at the victims this time. But none of us have a connection to Jazz. And what would Preethi's motive be?"

"Maybe she hates me so much that she's striking out at people I care about," he says, looking at Zora meaningfully. I half expect her to laugh, because the statement is so ridiculous, but she seems to swoon in response.

Dear lord . . .

"So, let me get this straight," Trissa says, jumping in before I have a chance. "Preethi somehow knew you were going to ask Zora to the dance, weeks before *you* did. And then she stole from herself and a bunch of other kids to . . . get back at you?"

Shrey attempts to double down. "You never know!"

Trissa, Alix, and I exchange the world's most incredulous look, and he crumples in response.

"All right," he says. "That's not a thing."

"So, what's next?" Alix asks. "The dance is tomorrow."

"Olivia works in the office during sixth period as a TA," I say. "I've got a test today in technology, but tomorrow I'll get a pass and see what I can find out."

"What am I going to do about this ransom thing?" Zora asks. "Honestly, I'm considering ignoring the demand and just reporting it to Mr. Lopez."

"If that's what you want, we can talk to Mr. Lopez now," I say. "But I don't think these notes will stop, even after you don't show up with the money. I still think your theft was personal. Like my pen."

"They do seem really different," Trissa agrees. "The Magicase is a limited edition, Jazz's suede jacket was by Clio Love, Emma's bag was a Swoon and Swank, and Juan's watch is a high-end brand—even if it's old."

Zora nods. "Xavier and Xo bracelets are nice, but I've seen other kids wearing them. And nobody wants my charms—they're only personal. Like Drew's pen. It's obvious that those thefts don't fit."

"The thief could have a more personal reason to target

you," I explain. "This happens a lot with perpetrators."

"Oooh, that's totally a thing," Alix says with an excited look on her face. "That's how a lot of criminals slip up and get caught, right?" Once again, I find my gaze locking on to Alix. This is, like, her *fifth* crime reference. A strange feeling bubbles up inside of me as I watch Alix tuck a strand of shiny black hair behind her ear.

"So, what should we do now?" Zora sighs, bringing my attention back. "I guess I could ask my parents for the money, but then they'll ask me why."

"We're only setting a trap," I say. "We could use paper, as long as it looks like it could be money. By the time the thief opens the card, our plan will already have worked."

"Wait, what trap? And what plan?" Zora asks. "Am I missing something?"

"I think this has to go down at the dance," I say with determination. "Setting a trap at the ransom drop is our best chance to get your bracelet back and solve this once and for all. With the right supplies, we can set a trap that will make us *positive* who the thief is."

Shrey looks at me with terror in his eyes. "What are you planning?"

"You know those dye packs they have at banks, or in the security tags at clothing stores?" I ask. "Well, I think we can make something similar."

"You want to make a dye pack explode when Olivia gets the money?" Trissa says, horrified. "Is that . . . legal?"

"Not a dye pack," I reassure her. "Something perfectly legal. A glitter bomb."

Zora's eyes go wide. "Oh! Alix did that to me once!"

Alix laughs. "Yep. It's like a present, but when you open it, it gets glitter all over you. It's sort of a prank-slash-present."

"Dad says that glitter *never* comes out," I explain. "This one time, I used it, and he said he was finding glitter on himself for *days*. Can you imagine what Olivia will look like if she gets glitter bombed? We would definitely know if it's her."

Zora smiles. "This could work. And you're sure you won't get in trouble?"

"No. I mean, I don't think so." A nervous feeling flutters across my stomach as I say it. I make a mental note to check the school rule handbook to make sure this couldn't possibly get us in trouble. Because, if I don't get suspended, I'm not ruining the Plan. Right?

"Are you sure?" Zora presses. "I don't want you to get busted because of me."

Trying to hide my uncertainty, I smile. "*Trust* me."

18

"**WE NEED TO GET THE** supplies for the glitter bomb today," I say as we start off campus a little while later. "There won't be time after school tomorrow. It's three thirty now and the art store is open until six. Does anyone need to call their parents to let them know?"

"Wait, now?" Shrey says. "I can't. I'm supposed to call Zora after we both get home."

I do a double take. "The Zora we saw, like, fifteen minutes ago?"

Trissa presses her lips together. "You don't think she'll understand? It kind of has to be tonight, since we won't have much time before the dance tomorrow."

Shrey slows to a stop, looking at both of us. "Can you two just do it? We really don't need all three of us to make a glitter bomb. You said so yourself. It's one store, easy-peasy."

I clench my jaw angrily. Shrey has been literally *zero* help these past few days. Ever since Zora said yes to the dance, he's basically been a boyfriend zombie. When he's not on the phone with Zora, he's texting her. Or talking about her. I guess I thought he'd be more interested in this case—it being his new *girlfriend's* mystery and all.

And, not for nothing, but he seems to have forgotten that my mom is here. Every time he called over the weekend, it was to rehash every detail of a phone conversation with Zora. Never to ask how it was going with me. Is this what crushes result in? Neglecting your friends and complete zombification?

The more time I spend with Zora, the more I realize that the weird feeling I keep getting isn't about Shrora. It's about Shrey. With every passing day, it feels like he's ditching us even more.

"Drew?" Shrey says when I don't answer right away. He finally seems to notice my expression. "Is that . . . okay?"

Yanking my backpack off, I grab my inhaler out of the side pocket and take a deep puff. Shrey looks at me even more nervously. He knows what that means.

"Sure, we can do it ourselves," I say in a low voice. "Like we've been doing everything else for this case."

"Wait, *what*?" Shrey says, holding his hands up.

"Um, think about the last few days, Shrey," I say sharply. "How many times have you bailed?"

I can see him mentally calculating. From the grimace on his face, it's obvious he knows I'm at least a little bit right. Still, he rushes to justify himself. "Okay, it's possible I haven't been *quite* as helpful as last time," he sputters.

"Understatement!" I exclaim.

"But I went with Trissa to find Jazz last week. And you were the one who told me to bail on Preethi. And . . . it's not like you haven't been doing fine without me!" Shrey blurts defensively. "I was never the real mystery-solver of this group anyway."

"We could still use your help!" Wheezing from the effort of yelling, I take a second puff of my inhaler and look at Trissa for help. A nervous expression takes over her face.

"You know how much I like Zora," Shrey continues, practically spitting the words out. "Do you not like her or something? Don't think I don't see you, rolling your eyes at me all day."

"All day?" I repeat, letting out a humorless laugh. "I didn't *see* you all day. Trissa and I have been running around campus *all day*, eliminating suspects, getting ransom notes for our prized possessions. It's like you don't even care that my Lita pen got stolen."

"But—" Shrey tries to interject.

"And how could you think I don't like Zora?" I cut him off. "I'm *literally* helping her."

Shrey kicks a rock into the street, his eyes cast downward. "I dunno. Maybe you're jealous or something. You're acting jealous right now."

"Shrey," Trissa breaks in. "You've got this all wrong. I don't think Drew is jealous." Still, her eyes flash back toward me and I can tell she isn't sure.

"Jealous, like I want *you* swooning all over me?" I scoff. "I don't think so."

"Whatever!" Shrey shouts, throwing his hands up. "I don't care who you like."

"I. Don't. Like. *ANYONE!*" I lose what cool I had left. Fortunately, the asthma medicine seems to have done the trick, so at least I'm breathing deeper now.

"Whatever," Shrey says.

"I'm not, like, this giant hormone monster like the rest of you!"

"Hey!" Trissa protests.

"Sorry," I say to her quickly. "I only mean . . . I'm not interested. I'm not interested in dancing or holding hands or anything like that." I break off and look right at Shrey. "Not with you, not with anyone. Okay?"

He nods weakly, and kicks another rock. "Yeah, fine. You know what? I'm going to make my own way home."

"Shrey," Trissa says, but he interrupts her.

"No." Shrey turns away, right as I think I see a glistening in his eyes. "I thought you guys would be happy for me. But you just want to make me feel bad. See you tomorrow or whatever."

I try to speak, but the words die in my throat. Right now, anything I say is going to sound mad. So, I let him walk away. When he crosses the street and disappears around the corner, I turn to Trissa.

"You're not a hormone monster," I say right away. "I'm sorry I said that."

"I know," she says glumly. "I mean, it's kind of true, but still. Don't drag me into your Drew and Shrey drama, okay? I told you after we met—I had kind of a rough year making friends when I started. I really don't want to lose you guys."

Blinking, I say, "I'm *really* sorry, Trissa. I didn't even think about that. I guess I saw red."

Looking at her nervously, I weigh what I should do. Trissa and I may not have known each other as long as Shrey and I have, but she's my best friend too. And she's a really good one. Am I getting so ballistic about Shrey that I'm pushing her away? I scramble for anything that will make her smile.

"I swear on Poe Dameron!" I exclaim. Trissa's eyes widen, and I make a crossing sign over my heart. "I swear on Poe Dameron I'll make up with Shrey and I'll work on my temper. Really, Trissa. This is a Poe promise."

She softens. "Don't say that unless you mean it."

"Look at my face right now." I widen my eyes as much as possible, leaning into her personal space, doing my best impression of a total creeper. "*Serioussssss,*" I hiss theatrically.

"All right, weirdo," she says with a laugh. "Only if we can hit Leclair's before we go to the art store. I need pastry."

"*Hundred* percent yes," I say, drooling at the thought.

It takes nearly a half hour, but we make our way to the downtown neighborhood strip. After liberating two croissants (chocolate for me, almond for Trissa), we head for Art's Arts. As you can imagine, the store is run by a guy named Art. So, his career was pretty much in the bag.

"Where can we find the glitter?" Trissa asks a store clerk when we walk in.

The teenager working the register points toward the left side of the store. "Aisle six," she says dully.

Trissa and I load up on glitter of the brightest, most thief-catching colors. I can't bring myself to walk down the aisle that sells fountain pen ink. It makes me too sad. But, spending the twenty that Dad gave me is for the best. Who knows if I'll even get my pen back from Olivia after this is over?

I pull off my backpack, digging around for the twenty. "Ugh!" I yell in frustration. "Dad and Shrey are right. My backpack is a nightmare. I had a twenty in here that should cover it . . ."

"I can pay for supplies," Trissa offers.

"Are you sure?"

"Let's just say I had a very merry Christmas this year," Trissa says, waggling her fingers excitedly. "Grammy and Pops went all out. I got money, new shirts, books . . ."

"Didn't you also get books at the book fair, too?"

Trissa turns and puts both her hands on my shoulders, as if she's dispensing words of great wisdom. "A girl can never have enough books, Drew. Remember that— always."

"Well, in any case, thanks," I say gratefully. "And I'll pay you back for half. I promise."

"I know where you live," Trissa jokes.

"Now let's go to stationery! I want to pick out the perfect greeting card for our ransom."

"You're weird," Trissa says with a laugh.

"*You're* weird," I reply.

She shrugs. "Agree to agree. Hey, can I ask you something?"

"You just did," I point out, grinning.

"No, I mean something personal. Is there someone you want to go to the dance with?"

"I think you know that the answer is no," I say carefully. Truthfully, when she asked, an image of one person popped into my mind. But I'm not ready to talk about that yet. Or think about it. Maybe ever. "Hey, you okay?" I ask her. "Are you really that bummed that you don't have a *date* date to the dance?"

She shrugs and tugs at the bottom of her sweater. "Eh, a little. But it's not like I tried. I don't know. I know I was the conductor of the Shrora train—"

"Ha!" I say. "Shrora! You've embraced it."

"Like a fungus, it grew on me," Trissa replies with a wry grin. "Anyway, I guess I wish I could find someone who likes me as much as Shrey likes Zora."

"That makes sense," I say.

"So, you're not . . . *jealous*? Of Shrey and Zora, I mean?"

"Like . . . do I want my very own couple mash-up name like 'Shrora'?"

She laughs. "No. I mean, do you like Shrey now?"

"No! I don't like Shrey now. Not like that."

Trissa fiddles with one of her braids. "The thing is, we're usually all together. Well, I know you turned Shrey down last fall. You told me that much. But I don't really know what your . . . *deal* is, because I didn't want to be pushy after that whole thing happened."

"My . . . deal," I repeat.

Trissa covers her face. "You know what I mean! I've told you my deal. I have an epic love of Poe, and there are exactly three boys who I find *not* gross at this school. I'll even tell you who they are: Simon Branden, Landon Agiers, and Neel Maharjan. Especially Simon Branden," she says, breaking off dreamily. Then, however, she snaps back to attention. "But I don't even know half of that for you!"

Oh. So *that's* what this is about.

Trissa lowers her voice and goes on. "I mean, is there a reason you don't want to talk to *me* about it? Because I'm cool, you know. Whoever you are, whoever you like, it's all good."

I'm about to answer when I accidentally knock into a petite woman crouched on her knees, stocking. She gives me a startled look, so I apologize, and lead Trissa down the other side of the aisle.

"Thanks for saying that," I say, steering her toward the cards. "I guess . . . I don't really know yet. The liking-people thing hasn't really kicked in for me. Yet?"

"But you do love Han Solo?"

I look around us furtively. "Yeah, I do love Han Solo. But, um, I also like girl characters." I blush so deep red I think I might die.

"That's cool!" Trissa insists. Leaning in conspiratori-ally, she waggles her eyebrows. "So, which girl characters are we talking about?"

My face must look like a giant tomato. "Fennec Shand from *The Mandalorian*?" I offer. "She's a recent one."

She gives me an approving look. "Oh, *totally* fair."

"Right?" I exclaim. "She's so cool. I don't really want a boyfriend *or* girlfriend at the moment, but I might make an exception if I met someone with super strength and stealth."

"So, you would marry Mr. Incredible?" Trissa jokes, shoving me.

"No, but maybe Frozone," I reply.

"Umm, he's married, you homewrecker!" Trissa teases and then slugs me playfully. Both of us collapse in laughter, and a wave of warmth flows through me. It feels good . . . until another emotion creeps up: guilt.

Is it wrong that I just basically told Trissa I might

be into both boys and girls, but I haven't officially told Shrey? I told him I might be somewhere in the middle when he asked if I like girls, but I hadn't been super clear. He's been my best friend since forever. Is it weird that it's so much easier to talk to Trissa about it? Ugh. Emotions and communication are hard.

Putting an abrupt stop to that line of thinking, I walk with Trissa toward the counter, armed with a few greeting cards and our glitter. I see a familiar face behind the register. Art's wife, Maeve. I know most twelve-year-olds probably don't know business owners by name, but that's what happens when you're a local bakery heiress.

"Hi, Maeve!" I say brightly.

"Hey, there, mini-Leclair," she says.

I hand her our haul and she lets out a thick scoff. "That's a lot of glitter," she says.

"It's, um, a special project," Trissa says. We exchange an amused look.

"Hey, can you take over the register?" Maeve calls out to someone behind us.

The same woman I'd tripped over rushes forward, practically stopping dead in her tracks when she sees me. She has curly black hair, bronze skin, and kind eyes.

OBSERVATIONS:

• The woman instinctively glances out the door, as if looking for someone who's missing.

• She looks at me like she knows me, even though I've never seen her before in my life. Almost like she's met me, but . . .

CONCLUSION:

I don't even have time to grasp the conclusion I'm reaching for, before I see it in front of me. The name tag on her apron reads: *Luna*.

19

A FEW HOURS LATER, I still haven't figured out how to ask Dad about the *Luna* situation.

The weird thing isn't even that he's dating someone. I mean, obviously it would have been ideal if he'd fallen madly in love with Lita Miyamoto (who, according to Twitter, remains tantalizingly single). But still, I want Dad to be happy. It's not the thought of him having a girlfriend that sets knots through my stomach.

It's that he hasn't told me. He told *Mom*, but he didn't tell me.

"Drew," he says, looking at me worriedly as he opens the refrigerator. "You're literally pacing in front of me. What's going on?"

"Well . . ." I consider my next words. There are a few roads for me to take here . . .

1) The Sneak Attack: "Hey, Dad! I ran into LUNA and she says hi!"

2) The San Francisco Switch (not really from San Francisco, but it sounds good): I tell Dad that Lita Miyamoto wrote me an email saying she wants to marry Dad, and then say: "That's not a problem for any reason, right?"

3) The Vague Bait: "You know, it would be really nice if you dated someone who worked in the craft industry . . . to satisfy my artisanal ink habit . . ."

Nope. All three of those might result in Dad choking on his bread, which would be suboptimal.

"I was only wondering what you're making for dinner tonight," I say.

"Burgers!" he tells me. "I even got lettuce wraps for the burgers for your mom so she could skip the bread."

"That's very nice of you," I say, awkwardly trying to find an opening to the Luna conversation. "You're a . . . thoughtful person."

He gives me a strange look. "Huh?"

"It's that—" I'm on the verge of going in for the kill when I hear a knock at the door. Mom. Did she have to choose tonight to break her trademark late streak?

"Hi, hi!" Mom announces after Dad lets her in. "How can I help?"

Hmm. Maybe I'll try again after she heads back to the hotel. I could lure him into it by suggesting we watch the new episode of *Painted Faces* and then, BOOM. He won't even know what hit him.

In the meantime, since Mom and Dad are making dinner and actually getting along, I decide to retreat to my room to work the case. Trissa and I had made three glitter bombs, one for the ransom and two backups just in case. After double-checking that all three are safely tucked inside my desk drawer, I meander toward my crime board.

First, I review my profile of Olivia from the weekend:

OLIVIA FERNANDA CAMPOS

MEANS: Has access to the lockers, like everyone

MOTIVE: Olivia's friends have money, and are known for spending it. She could be stealing to keep up with their lifestyle. Olivia used to be friends with Zora Scurlock. Olivia could know Zora enough to believe she would be intimidated into paying a ransom.

OPPORTUNITY: Anyone can walk into the

locker area with a pass, and Olivia
shares a PE period with Zora.
COUNTERPOINT: Most of the victims
reported using their locks. Method of
getting in without breaking the locks
unknown.

After pinning up my remaining notes, I mock up a drawing of the multipurpose room as it will be decorated for the Wonderland dance. I include where each of us will be when Zora makes the dead drop, as well as the routes to the girls' bathroom. Smiling, I sketch a little picture of a sad figure, carrying a bag of money and covered in glitter.

Then, I grab my phone for a quick scroll of the "Badgers Ahoy!" Instagram account. I haven't seen anything pop up in the past week, but it's worth looking. Who knows, maybe Alix was right about Olivia selling the stolen items, and I could find a picture of someone else with Juan's watch, or Emma's bag. Unfortunately, nothing jumps out at me. Most of the posts are about the Wonderland dance—who's going with who, and whether it's going to be "epic."

Hmmm. I think for a moment, and then type in *#badgersahoy* just to see if I missed anything from students' personal accounts. I only follow "Badgers Ahoy!" because of the Ella Baker Shade mystery. Other than that, I don't follow many people. When I see the most recent post, I spring upright.

Whoa.

The post is a picture of the PE lockers, with one wide-open in the center. Items are strewn around inside, so it definitely looks like our thief. The text reads:

OK, WHO TOOK MY RETRO ROYALE JORDANS????? #ellabakerbadgers #badgersahoy #stealingisacrime

It's from Brian Wu. As in, Connor's new *boyfriend*, Brian Wu.

Scrambling, I call Connor.

"Drew! I was *just* about to call you," he answers without saying hello.

"About Brian's . . ." I trail off, realizing I have no idea what "Retro Royale" Jordans are. "Erm, stolen items?"

"He saved up for literally a year to buy the Retro Royale Jordans," Connor wails. "He almost never wears them to school, but then Javier—the guy who plays the Duke of Weselton in *Frozen*—totally called him out. He said Brian was lying about getting them over break. The guy is basically Weaseltown himself."

"Umm . . ." I close my eyes, still not sure what he's talking about, save for the *Frozen* characters. Can I Google this fast enough? "Yes," I say stiffly. "Yes! I see that Jordans are a very popular brand of sneakers, released for Michael Jordan in 1984 . . ."

"Are you reading a Wikipedia article right now?" Connor asks.

"Okay, yes!" I admit. "I had no idea that fancy sneakers are a thing."

He laughs. "Nike releases a ton of them, but some are pricier, or harder to get. It's okay. I know you're more into crime scenes than fashion athletic wear."

"That's true."

"Hey, but speaking of which," Connor goes on. "Is this the 'business' you were talking about the other day? Even before Brian's sneakers got snatched, I started hearing kids talking. People are really nervous about their stuff right now. Brian almost wore his Jordans in PE until he saw all the mud on the track."

"It is," I confirm. "Zora Scurlock asked me to look into her missing bracelet, and all of these other thefts started popping up."

"Do you know who did it yet?" Connor asks breathlessly.

Staring at the crime board, now showing Olivia's profile pinned to the center, I say, "I think I do. I just have to prove it."

Connor and I talk for another few minutes, and I gather as much information as I can secondhand. I figure I can try to talk to Brian tomorrow but, even if I don't see him, our dance plan is ready to go.

I'm so focused on taking notes after the phone call that when a little *bing!* erupts from my phone, I jump in surprise.

Ugh. It's Shrey. Even though I see the words "I'm sorry" in the notification banner, I still toss my phone on my bed.

"Sweetheart?" My mom's head pokes through the doorway the moment I chuck it against the pillow. "Dinner is ready in a few. You okay?" she asks, gesturing to my phone.

"Oh!" I say with a surprised laugh. "Yeah. Just avoiding Shrey."

Oh, lord.

Why did I have to say that? Whenever Mom catches a whiff of school or friend drama, she asks a million questions. Well, I suppose she already knows about the Shrey thing, since Dad blabbed. And Mom has been surprisingly supportive since our coffee date. Maybe she would actually be a good person to talk to about this.

"Shrey has been weird off and on since the kissing thing," I explain shakily, hoping this won't turn into a huge conversation. "He doesn't get that I don't want to date anyone."

She rests a hand on my shoulder. "Because you're interested in your other friend?" she asks. "Trissa, right?"

I press my lips together in annoyance. Shrey had basically accused me of the same thing in the fall. Is my making a new friend so strange that *everyone* thinks I must be in love with them or something?

"I'm not interested in Trissa that way. And she likes boys, by the way," I say, a little more intensely than I mean to.

"Oh. Okay, then," Mom says. She lets out a silky laugh. "I'm sorry. I'm probably being really awkward about this right now. I don't want you to think I wouldn't accept you, whoever you like. I only want to know about it."

That was actually really nice, so I offer her a wan smile. "I get it," I say. "But, can I be honest?"

"Of course!"

I take in a long breath, trying to summon Lita Miyamoto–level strength as I say, "I heard you talking to Dad about it. And, even though you *say* you would accept me either way, I still get the feeling you'd be weird if I liked a girl."

She bristles. "I'm not! I mean . . ." She looks pensive, like she can't figure out how to proceed. "The only reason I'm concerned is that people got picked on for that when I was in school."

"In, like, the late 1990s?" I scoff. "Yeah. Things are different now. I'm not saying no one gets picked on, but it's different."

Mom looks a little bit affronted but takes a deep breath. "I know. I'm sorry, honey. I know I get things wrong sometimes. But I am trying."

She leans forward for a hug and, after a poignant delay, I accept it. It's been so long since we've hugged that I forgot how nice it feels.

"You really wouldn't care?" I asked. "If I end up liking girls, I mean."

"I only care about you being happy," she says, then brushes a tear from her eye. "Oh, sweetie. I've missed you so much."

The admission hits me like a knife to the gut. But . . . not in a bad way? I've been spending the last few months *so* sure that she wasn't missing me. I thought she was parasailing, and snorkeling, and living it up in Kauai without the burden of an oddball daughter at her side.

I've been spending so long pretending that I didn't miss *her* that it never occurred to me that she might miss *me*.

"Me too," I say, feeling the annoying heat of tears at the back of my eyes.

"So, can I ask a favor?" Mom says after we both pull away.

I feel a bit hesitant, like at any moment the other shoe is going to drop. But, really, how many shoes can there be? "Sure," I say slowly.

"I know you kind of ghosted me about the shopping trip. And I get that. Shopping trips have never been perfect for us. But can I help you pick out an outfit for the Wonderland dance? I have to be honest; I'm dying to do it. It's sort of a mom rite of passage."

"Sure, Mom," I say with relief. Letting her pick something from my closet will be way better than shopping. "Dad's not exactly fashion-forward, so I could probably use the help."

Mom laughs. "You think? The other day, he was wearing maroon and orange *together*." She sets her phone down and heads for my closet to rifle through the choices.

For half a second, I almost burst out with a million questions. Some of them are about Dad and Luna, and some are about what she likes about Mr. Clark, who seems like a dull beige blob. But one question—*If you miss me so much, why did you leave?*—nags at me until I feel like I might burst. In spite of this, I stay quiet as she digs through my clothes. Things are going too well for me to sour the moment with my trademark honesty.

"Leggings, legging, leggings. Is this all you wear other than your school uniform?" Mom grouses.

"They're comfortable," I say with a shrug.

"What about the shirt you wore the other day?" She holds it up, next to a maxi skirt from the back of my closet. "This could be cute. Ooh, never mind. This is the one." Mom drops the blouse and grabs a long-forgotten dress from the back of my closet. It's a black skater dress, with a tiny border of embroidered Kaonashi from *Spirited Away*. I actually remember looking good in that dress.

"Okay. This one isn't bad," I say, grabbing the dress.

"Success!" she shouts, shaking her fists.

"Thanks, Mom," I say genuinely. "I do like this. And . . ." I trail off, summoning a different kind of courage to say the next words. "It's been nice . . . um, spending time with you again."

Her smile glows. "That's why I'm here, sweetheart. So . . . let's see the dress! Can you try it on and show me?"

"Um, sure?" I say. Fashion shows have never really been my thing, but I know Mom likes it. When we'd have good days—before she left—she would love to try on all of her finds from Nordstrom Rack or Marshalls.

"Great! I'll tell your dad we'll be just a few minutes longer for dinner." She ducks outside the door, and I quickly slip out of my clothes and into the dress.

Another *bing!* sounds from my phone, and I groan. Shrey, again?

When I read the banner notification on the screen, I'm confused at first. This wasn't what he texted me last. But it only takes a few seconds before I realize my mistake. I picked up Mom's phone, not mine. Mine is still tossed at the back of my bed, by my pillow. The moment I grab it, of course, the whole screen lights up with the previous messages. Mom's phone is set on "lift to wake" like it always is.

When I see all the messages that came before, a dull ache spreads across my chest, like I got hit square in the chest. I draw in a shaky breath and squeeze my eyes shut, hoping to block out what I just read. But I can't. Prying one eye open, I look at it again:

SMS; Jenn, Dustin

> **DUSTIN:** Hey, baby. I miss you so much. Did you talk to Sam about signing the papers early yet?
>
> **JENN:** I'm talking to him tonight before I leave.

DUSTIN: If there's no contest, we can wrap up the divorce by next month. It doesn't have to take so long. Make sure you ask him tonight, okay?

JENN: That's why I'm here. 😔

DUSTIN: K sweetie talk later 😔

I read it once more, a wave of tears coming before I can stop them.

That's why I'm here.

Not to see me. Not to reconnect after how we left things last year. To get divorced faster. That's why she's here.

A light knock sounds at my door, and I scramble to grab the tissues. "Hold on a second!" I call out. After dabbing at my face for a minute and taking a few breaths, I call back out to her.

"Oh, sweetheart! You look amazing!" she gushes. "See, *this* is what school is all about."

I flinch when she rushes forward and spins me around.

"Thanks for letting me help," she goes on. "I'll miss seeing you off tomorrow, but I'm glad I get to be a part of your special night in some way."

I pinch my lips into a tight smile. "Yeah, Mom. That's why you're here."

20

~~Dear Mom,~~
~~Why can't you~~

~~Dear Mother . . .~~

~~Dear Ms. Jennifer Leclair,~~
~~I am writing to officially request~~

To Whom It May Concern . . .

"UGH!" I SLAM MY NOTEBOOK shut, imagining flinging it across the room, but thinking better of it. By lunch the next day, I've started at least ten letters to my mother. If she can indeed call herself that. At one point,

I'd even written a letter like the one Lita Miyamoto wrote to Masterpiece Man:

> You thought you could get away with it. You thought you could hide behind your spa days and mother-daughter fashion shows, acting like you were here for me. But you never thought I'd get the evidence, did you? You weren't here for me. You were never here at all.

Of course, I could never send that. The last time I told Mom what I thought of her, it did *not* go well. A little gurgle sounds from my midsection and I shift uncomfortably, holding my stomach. Making everything worse is the fact that all of my mom-induced stress has settled right in my gut. Which, of course, has sent me into a whole different spiral, and forced me to ask myself the question:

If I get this way every time I'm stressed, I wonder, *how am I supposed to be a profiler?*

Can I even be in the FBI with chronic illnesses? Wouldn't it be frowned upon to use my inhaler or start, like, randomly farting at a crime scene?

So, to sum up, not only do I have unpredictable bodily functions—I have too many unpredictable bodily functions to ever realize my dream. Which would make Mom *super* happy, I'm sure. Awesome.

"Um, hey?" Shrey's voice breaks into my thoughts.

I turn to face him, craning my neck to see if Trissa is trailing behind.

"Trissa said you were eating your lunch here," Shrey says. "I told her I wanted to talk to you," he explains, seeing my expression.

"Okay." I glance down to make sure I've actually closed my notebook. Eventually, I'll fill Shrey in on the latest Mom development, but I don't feel like talking about it now.

"Look, I'm really sorry."

"I *don't* hate Zora," I say.

"I know. Can I tell you the truth?"

"Always."

Shrey looks at me sheepishly. "You were mad at me. And I think I was so mad that *you* were mad that I said a bunch of stuff I don't even mean. Does that make sense?"

"It sounded like you meant it," I say bluntly.

He sighs. "I don't know why I said all that. I know that you're not jealous, but I guess . . . I don't know. There's a lot I feel like I don't know anymore."

As annoying as Shrey has been, I know I can't stay mad at him. For one, I know deep down that I've been a little absorbed in this mystery. Maybe a little obsessive. Especially when I know that him getting a girlfriend is a big deal for him. He's a romance guy.

Second, of course, there's the weird twinge I keep getting about him *having* said girlfriend. The idea of *telling* him all that makes me want to crawl under a rock. Still, he's my best friend.

"I think I was jealous!" I practically shout before I can chicken out. When his jaw drops, I rush to add, "Not like you were saying yesterday, though. I really like Zora. But maybe I didn't really get that time with *her* would also mean time away from us. Well, um, from *me*. Does that sound ridiculous?"

"No," Shrey says, kicking a rock. "I felt that way in October when we met Trissa. I know I tried to make it sound like you might *like* like her, but I don't know if I believed that. I was only jealous that you were spending time with her outside of me."

"And . . ." Tears come to my eyes before I can stop them. "I didn't want you to leave me. Enough people leave me. Okay?"

Shrey reaches in to hug me and I actually let him. "You have the best lunches," he says. "I would *never* bail on you."

I let out a thick laugh. He's joking, of course, but I

know what he really means.

"Same. You're my best friend. And I'm sorry I got annoyed when you were talking about Zora. I know that having a girlfriend is really big for you. I promise you can tell me anything and I'll listen. *Without* the eye-rolls."

I suddenly flush, thinking about the conversation I had with Trissa yesterday, and the guilt I had over not telling Shrey. Then, I think about the texts I'd seen on Mom's phone. A few months ago, Shrey would have been the *first* person I'd tell about Mom stuff. He would understand.

I clear my throat, readying myself to start a conversation I'm not really prepared for, when he blurts, "So, do you forgive me? For being a clueless friend *and* totally useless to the Jedi Detective Agency? I promise, as of today, I'm all in."

I let out a relieved laugh, but then cross my arms theatrically. "*Fine*. But next time I'll probably just murder you. Or kick you a lot. Followed by the murder. And maybe some more kicking."

Shrey smirks. "That's fair. Avoid the face, though. That's my moneymaker."

He slides down next to me, giving me a ridiculous duck face. We both burst into laughter.

I almost open my mouth again to tell him about everything, but a soft crackling nearby startles us both. When we glance up, Zora and Alix are looking down at us.

"Um, hi!" Zora says, casting a look between us. "Are we interrupting?"

"No! Never!" Shrey practically shouts as he scrambles to stand up.

I stand up too, rolling my eyes and brushing a few dry leaves off my sweats. "What Shrey means is that you're always welcome. And, besides, we were about to talk about the case."

"Did you hear about Brian?" Alix asks. She shakes her head. "He said he'll never be able to afford replacing those Jordans."

I look at her with surprise. "How did you find out? Were you looking at Instagram too?"

"We heard Brian talking to Vice Principal Lopez this morning," Zora explains.

"I talked to him before," I tell them. "And Connor last night. It's the same MO. The thief took his shoes, but left everything else behind. No ransom note, but everything else fits." I break off, murmuring, "He didn't tell me that he reported it, though. I wonder if this is going to ramp up fast. I hope we can solve this case tonight. And that Vice Principal Lopez will be happy this time when we do."

Truthfully, this shoe theft is throwing me. Olivia is *definitely* not wearing men's Jordans. And she's not reselling the items, at least on any of the sites we've been checking. Is it possible she's stealing these things just to take them? I'd learned about the word "kleptomania" in one of my crime books. Maybe it's a compulsion. Or maybe she really *is* like the Masterpiece Man. Could she be taking these things just to deprive people of them? With Olivia's most likely motive being money, a lot of this doesn't make sense.

I don't tell the others how uneasy I'm feeling, though. Zora needs to have confidence going into this ransom drop, and I don't want her to know how lost I'm feeling in the noise of this case.

"Do we have everything we need for tonight?" Alix asks. She jangles her wrist, making a melodic sound.

For a second, my memory snags on something. I look between Alix and Zora. "You said one of the charms on your missing bracelet was inscribed. Does Alix have the same exact charms?"

They trade a secret smile that reminds me of the week before.

"I like to hand inscribe my own charms," Zora says.

"My rock dorkiness extends to metals. I inscribed some for me and Alix. They say 'F4.' It stands for 'French-fry friends forever.' Kind of an inside joke thing."

"Ah, got it," I say, frowning. That might explain the look they'd shared, but something still bothers me. It feels like I'm straining to retrieve a thought, but can't quite catch it. "Alix, do you ever keep *your* bracelet in the lockers?"

Alix shakes her head. "Nope. I leave my jewelry on during PE. I also like to wear sweats on PE days so I don't have to change. Truth is, I don't really use the lockers."

That explains why Alix's bracelet wouldn't be stolen. But something was still bothering me.

"So," Alix prods again. "Can I help at all? You know, with the plan?"

After shaking off the uneasy feeling, I say, "I think we're good. Trissa and I made three cards with glitter bombs, just in case we need a backup. We can slip the money inside the envelope." I take out my phone to show her a picture of our bomb-making craft.

"Thank-you cards?" Alix says with a laugh. "Nice touch."

"Yep," I reply, grinning wickedly. "I'm betting our thief will be curious enough to open it. After all, it's not every day you get a thank-you card from your victim."

21

ONCE I GET TO TECHNOLOGY class, it only takes five minutes and a series of well-placed moans to end up in front of Ms. Tuitasi's desk.

For a second, I think I'll have a problem when Ethan Navarez starts muttering about how "fake" I sound. Ethan has only been back in class a few weeks—after spending the rest of fall semester in a Digital Citizenship tutorial—but he's basically been glaring at me the whole time. This is the first time he's spoken, though.

It makes me wonder how Lita Miyamoto would feel, having to sit in class with the perpetrators she catches.

Probably pretty awkward.

Fortunately, Ms. Tuitasi doesn't seem to notice Ethan. "You take all the rest you need," she tells me, tucking a purple strand of hair behind her ear. "Feel better, okay?"

I hold my stomach and walk slowly from the room. I commit to the slow, pained lurching until I get to the stairway. I hate lying in general, but especially about my chronic illnesses. Since I legitimately *have* stomach issues, this will probably cost me later. With my luck, I'll get so stressed about lying that it'll bring on the symptoms I'm faking.

Oh well. Since seeing Mom's texts last night, I've had a stomachache anyway. Might as well lean all the way in.

"Uhhhhhh," I moan as I walk into the office.

"Oh no!" an unfamiliar woman says, putting a hand to her face.

I look both ways, and back at the woman. "Where's Ms. Marika?"

"I'm subbing in for her today," the woman explains. "She had to take her grandson to an appointment. I'm Ms. Walker. Why don't you go ahead and lie down. If you're not feeling better in an hour, we'll call your mom."

I almost correct the assumption, but decide against it. Honestly, it's a relief that Ms. Marika isn't here today, since she still doesn't trust me in the office after I broke into the file room last semester to get evidence. This way I don't have to do quite as much acting.

I walk into the nurse's station—thankfully, seconds

before I see Olivia Campos walk behind the desk with a big stack of papers.

"Are you done with those flyers, dear?" I hear Ms. Walker ask.

"Yes, ma'am!" Olivia says brightly. She sits down in the office chair in the corner and turns toward a computer screen.

I angle myself on the couch so that I can see through the window but stay partially obscured from Olivia's seat. The perfect spot for observation.

"Thanks, dear," Ms. Walker says. "You can do homework for now. I'll let you know when I have a new project for you."

"All right," Olivia responds, her voice somewhat muffled.

I move to lean closer to the door, when a sharp pain snakes its way across my belly. *Oof, here comes the cramping. My payment for lying.*

Still, I manage to sit up, stretching as high as possible, and peer through the glass. Right now, Olivia is just staring at a computer screen. It's hard to tell exactly what she's doing. It could be math, or coding. But it doesn't look like the student email server, or like she's writing a paper.

It's probably nothing, I tell myself despondently.

Another non-clue that leads nowhere.

But then Olivia glances furtively at Ms. Walker, her eyes flicking toward the screen.

OBSERVATIONS:

- Olivia twists the monitor so it's blocked from view.
- She glances back and forth.
- She discreetly pulls out her phone and points it at the screen until I hear a faint *snap*.

CONCLUSION: Olivia is looking at something she shouldn't, and taking pictures of it with her phone.

Interesting. Maybe she's logged into the school server? Or she found a way to get into Emma's file? I can't look away. If only I could get Ms. Walker to leave . . .

"Excuse me." A familiar voice cuts into my plotting. "My teacher sent me to lie down in the nurse's station, but I'm also supposed to give you this." Alix hands a note to Ms. Walker and turns to face me, winking obviously.

Wait, what is *Alix* doing here?

"Thank you," Ms. Walker says. The skin between her brows crinkles like she's worried. "She needs copies. Oh dear. I don't think I remember how to work the machine. Olivia, sweetheart. Can you run these copies for me?"

Olivia looks up at her, panicked. "Well, um . . . I'm just finishing something up. If you'll let me—"

"You can come back to your gossip sites later. Come on. Help an old woman." Ms. Walker rushes Olivia out of her chair. Olivia moves to click the mouse, but I can't tell if she was able to close anything before she's up. The consternated look on her face before she disappears through the door tells me she might have missed something.

"Hey," Alix whispers, ducking into the nurse's office and sitting next to me. "So . . . remember how I wanted to help?"

"Yeah?"

"Well, I thought you could use a wingman. Or wingwoman. Wing . . . girl?" She giggles, and her messy black bun flops forward.

I look out at the office again. "I was going to find a way to check Olivia's computer screen. But I admit, I'm kind of persona non grata in the office."

"After the file room incident?" she fills in. "I heard.

Well, let me do it, then!"

I cock an eyebrow at her. "You up for it?"

Alix cracks her knuckles and grins. "Oh, I was born ready. After school, I totally want to be an investigative journalist."

I can't help but take a moment to ask, "Really? What topic?"

"Social justice," she says. "I basically want to be that podcaster who gets someone out of prison, and then catches the guy who *really* did the crime."

My jaw drops. "Wait, really?"

Alix smiles and rests a hand on my arm. "You're not the only one who's into that stuff, Leclair. I waffle."

"*C-crime and Waffles?*" I sputter.

She nods and, for the first time in a long time, I feel totally speechless.

An image flashes in my mind before I can process what I'm thinking. It's Alix and me as roommates in an apartment. I would be in the FBI, of course, and she would be rocking the investigation podcast life . . .

Wait. Isn't this usually my go-to daydream with made-up people?

"Leclair? You with me?" Alix smiles as she makes a point of exaggeratingly waving her hands in front of her face.

OBSERVATIONS:

- My stomach suddenly feels weird in a good way.
- My pulse is significantly faster than it was a few minutes ago.

CONCLUSION: Some kind of rapid-onset social disorder?

"Yes!" I blurt awkwardly. "Um . . . I mean. Yeah."

"Okay," Alix says. She gives me a mischievous look. "Watch this."

"Ms. Walker," Alix moans. "I'm so sorry, but can I use the phone really fast?"

Ms. Walker lowers her glasses. "Anything wrong, dear?"

Alix gives me a split-second wicked look and then turns back. "Um, this is embarrassing. I need to call my mom and tell her to pick up some medicine for . . . *lady* issues."

"Of course!" Ms. Walker says. She sweeps a hand at the phone on Olivia's desk.

I'm literally on the edge of my seat, watching Alix

pretend to use the phone. She grabs the mouse and . . .

"Hey, Mom," Alix says. "I really need more of, you know, that *thing*." She pauses, nodding. "Yeah. Thanks. I love you too, Mom."

Wow. True commitment to acting. Not bad.

As she slips back through the door and sits down next to me, her eyes sparkle brightly. "Well, looks like little miss *Olivia* forgot to close the file she was looking at."

"And?"

Alix beams from ear to ear. "You know how we all get locks at the beginning of the year? Well, she was in a file that has *all* the combinations. Like, for each student who checked out a lock." She leans back and crosses her arms behind her neck. "How about that?" she says. "I think I found our smoking gun."

22

A FEW HOURS LATER, I find myself with (1) evidence, and (2) a plan (see: glitter bombs). But all I can seem to think about is that moment I had with Alix in the office.

Or . . . was it a *moment* at all? I don't know about these things. But I did start to think about her in a way that I never think about real people.

Wait.

Is this the hormone-monster cult? Did they recruit me and I didn't even know it? At least I'm not thinking about kissing yet. Is that the final stage?

I suddenly feel *really* bad about giving Shrey and Trissa a hard time. Once this cult gets you, it really gets you.

"Okay, let's figure out a timeline," Dad says, interrupting my internal monologue. "We have two hours before you need to be at the dance, right?"

"Right," I murmur.

"And I'll pick Trissa up at five forty-five? So that really means we have an hour. Do you want me to call your mom? She said you two had so much fun trying on clothes last night."

He pulls out his phone and scrolls like he's about to do it. So, I do the only thing I can think of. I scream "NO!" at the top of my lungs and smack his phone out of his hands.

For an aspiring detective, I'm not what you'd call "inconspicuous."

Dad stands staring between the phone on the floor and his empty hands, before he starts laughing. "What the heck?"

"Um . . . no Mom. Okay?"

"Okay, Captain Calm." He retrieves his phone from the ground and inspects it for cracks. "No Mom tonight. But we're having a last dinner with her tomorrow, and then we'll drive her to the airport on Friday. Does that sound good?"

I squeeze my eyes shut. It doesn't sound good. It sounds *terrible*. My mom is a total liar. I'm probably about to get in trouble again and ruin the Plan. And I may well be in the early stages of transforming into a hormone monster. Awesome.

"Drew," Dad says. His expression is still light, but his forehead is starting to crease with worry when I still don't reply. "Is everything okay?"

So, here's the thing. All my life, I've tried to shut down my emotions. It was actually super helpful in elementary school, because you can't bully someone who doesn't care. But last year Dad pointed out that my whole "no emotion" experiment led to some . . . *unhealthy* behavior.

Have I been doing it again this week? Probably. I haven't talked to Dad about Luna, or about the texts I saw on Mom's phone last night.

And then there's Alix.

But *no*. I can't talk about that. Maybe things will go better at the dead drop tonight if I get one of these things off my chest, though.

"Dad?" I begin tentatively.

"Yes?"

"Can you tell me about Luna now . . . please?"

His body tenses, and he gazes down at me with a look of total shock. "How did you . . . ? I mean, how long have you . . . ?"

I sit up, crossing my arms. "How long have I known about *Luna*, you mean?"

"Um." His eyes are bugging out, and he looks like he can't form words yet, so I go on.

"Well, I've known something was up since that night at the bakery last week. Then, I overheard you and Mom fighting on Friday, and she mentioned your girlfriend."

"Okay, but . . . you said . . . Luna," he fumbles.

I give him a prim look. "Well, what was I supposed to do? You weren't telling me about her, so I had to interrogate Mom using Lita Miyamoto's second questioning style."

"'Pretend you already know everything,'" Dad fills in the rest, moaning with realization.

"Right. And *she* said the name Luna. But I didn't know what she looked like until—"

"Until you ran into her at Art's," Dad finishes my sentence again. "She told me that she saw you. I've shown her about a million pictures, so she recognized you the second you walked in."

"She didn't give you away," I assure him. "You *totally* didn't cover your tracks."

"I wasn't trying to!"

"But then why did you tell Mom?" I ask. "Why her and not me?"

He cleans his glasses. *Oof.*

"Your mom and I are in a place where we have to be

very honest with each other. I had to let her know that I was planning on asking Luna out on a date, but I didn't want to tell you until I was sure it was happening. Does that make any sense?"

I don't really get what's going on with him and Mom, but I can relate to the idea of keeping something private until it's figured out. Especially after today.

I shrug in response. "I guess. But can you tell me *now*? Just promise me she's not beige. I don't think I could handle that."

"She's one of us," Dad says mysteriously.

I straighten. "What do you mean? Come on, Dad, you've got to give me *something*."

A satisfied smirk spreads over his face. He takes his phone back out and scrolls up in what looks like his texting app. Then, he shows me a picture.

Before I even see Luna, I shout, "But that's Gerald and Max! This is from the *Game Over* live podcast show last month!"

"And Luna," he says, pointing to the woman next to them. Luna is beaming like it's the best day of her life, her black curls falling over her shoulders. Behind them is a cardboard cutout with the *Game Over* logo— an illustrated take on Masterpiece Man made of puzzle pieces.

"Wait, does that mean . . ." I sputter.

"Yes. She is a fan of true crime."

My eyes speak before I can. "Dad . . . that's the dream!"

"I know!" he says giddily.

He pulls me in to nestle against his shoulder on the couch, and it makes me feel safe. Like I'm a little kid again.

A little kid with a pack of glitter bombs and an elaborate plan to take down a school thief.

The thought rattles me out of my cocoon.

"Okay, I should get ready," I tell Dad, sitting upright. "I've got . . . accessories to prepare."

He narrows his eyes. "Is that code for checking your crime board?"

"What?" I can practically feel my face turn pink.

"Oh, I see you," he says, laughing. "Look, as long as there's no breaking and entering—"

"There isn't, I swear. We're only finding Shrey's girlfriend's bracelet."

Because Zora's bracelet is still my top priority! Or . . . is it?

Okay, it's priority number *two* now, if I'm being totally honest. Being without the Lita pen makes me feel incomplete in a way I can't seem to shake. Almost as if

I've lost my arm or something. And isn't an *arm* more important than a bracelet?

"Well, well, well," Dad says. "The girl he liked is a girlfriend now?"

"Full couple," I confirm.

"Good for Shrey," he says, looking impressed "But, anyway. If anything goes south, you have my number. You got it? Anything. I can run a dozen croissants over there with fifteen—no, *ten* minutes' notice!"

"Got it," I say, giggling. I give him one more bear hug, and then dash down the hallway.

Because I know I'll get distracted with other preparations, I get dressed first. The stretchy Kaonashi skater dress slips over my head easily, and a pair of black lace-up boots is the perfect finishing touch.

"Might have to do something about this," I murmur to myself, grasping a chunk of my thick auburn hair. I sit down, staring at my reflection in the mirror. I'm not much of a fashion person most days. But this is also my first dance. I should look a little more put together than most days, when I let my hair frizz out defiantly until it looks like a giant puffy triangle. A pufftrangle. Tripuffle. Yeah.

Remembering the curl cream that Mom got me last year for my birthday, I run to the bathroom. After about twenty minutes of primping, I find myself standing next to the full-length mirror in my closet. My waves are not a tripuffle. They make me look like a girl in a hair product commercial.

I . . . look *good*.

It's not like I've ever thought of myself as ugly—despite Alicia, Emma, and Brie telling me that I was all through grade school. I guess I didn't think of myself as anything at all. Back in October, when Shrey told me he liked me, part of me was surprised. I never thought of myself as someone who *would* be liked in that way. But I figured that's because I wasn't interested in that.

Now, taking in my reflection . . . I guess I can almost see why someone would like me. In *that* way. This is so weird.

It's usually hard to find dresses that work, since I have skinny limbs and a round stomach. Most days, I feel a bit like an apple with little toothpicks sticking out. But this dress feels like it's meant for me. And the boots give the whole look a dash of rebellion, so I don't feel that I'm dressing like everyone else.

On a whim, I grab an untouched brown leather jacket from the back of my closet. It was Mom's Christmas present last month, and I'd stubbornly refused to wear it since she didn't bother to come home. But, it's actually really nice. I'm not a fancy person, but I have to admit it looks great with the dress.

Once again, Alix flashes in my head. It must be because I've seen her wear a jacket like this. Right? Or maybe because she *keeps* popping into my head for no reason all of a sudden. Either way, it makes me wonder what she'll wear tonight. And what she'll think of what I'm wearing. *Oof.*

"Wow," Dad says, appearing behind me. "You look really great. Are you sure this isn't a *dance* dance?"

I laugh. "No. It's just a group hang."

Even as I say it, I think of Alix yet again. What is *wrong* with me? Is this what a crush feels like? Because, honestly, it does feel like I'm getting flattened by an elephant.

Whatever. I need to keep my mind on one mystery at a time.

"Are you ready to go?" Dad asks, looking a little teary.

I pick up my black canvas messenger bag adorned with patches from all of my favorite pop-culture fandoms. Tucked inside are three glitter bombs, my notebooks, and a handheld recorder.

What *every* girl needs for her first real dance.

"Yep," I say, grinning at him. "I'm ready."

23

THE WONDERLAND STING (A.K.A. SUPER-SECRET TRAP)!

STEP ONE: Trissa and I meet up with Alix before the dance at 6:00 p.m.

STEP TWO: We watch as Shrey and Zora arrive, noting any suspicious activity.

STEP THREE: Alix and I hide in one of the four bathroom stalls while Zora does the ransom drop at 6:45 p.m.

STEP FOUR: Olivia emerges, all glittery, and confesses her crimes in front of the assembled students.

STEP FIVE: ~~Drew is hailed as a hero and everyone cheers.~~ Victory high fives all around!

"I TAKE BACK EVERYTHING I said about the yeti a minute ago," I say as Trissa, Alix, and I walk into the multipurpose room and behold the giant creature. "He's . . ."

"Frightening?" Trissa offers.

I shake my head. "I watch serial killer documentaries to fall asleep, so . . . no."

"Tacky?" Trissa offers.

"Never," I say, transfixed.

"Majestic," Alix says.

I snap my fingers, grinning at her. "That's the one."

I wasn't wrong about Alix having a good outfit for the dance. She wears a maroon dress and a bomber jacket with a water element patch. Effortlessly cool. Trissa looks great, too. She's abandoned her beloved flip sequins for the night and is wearing a mint-green strapless dress with cascading ruffles.

Actually, being here with both of them feels totally normal. Not at all like I'm transforming into any kind of monster. Maybe that was a blip—

"Your dress is awesome, by the way," Alix tells me. She points to my neckline. That's the Kaonashi, right?"

My face temperature suddenly increases by fifty degrees. So . . . maybe not.

"Uhhh, yeah," I fumble. "*Kiki's Delivery Service* is probably my favorite, but I like *Spirited Away.*"

"Very cool," Alix says.

I smile, but then grimace as I squirm in my coat. "I wish *I* was cool. It's weirdly hot for January."

"You should drop your jacket off in the back," Trissa suggests. "Mr. Crohner is on coat check in the hallway."

"Okay, but I'm not leaving my bag," I insist. "I've got all the supplies I need here."

"Like a detective kit?" Alix asks.

"Let's just say that Drew's dad named her after Nancy Drew," Trissa jokes. "And she learned to always come prepared."

Alix gives me an approving look and, once again, I feel my stomach do somersaults. Is this what people call butterflies? It doesn't feel that way to me. More like Cirque du Soleil is rehearsing in my abdomen. Which is better than a swarm of insects, but not by much.

"That's me." My face is producing heat at an alarming rate. "Um, I'll see you in a few."

"We'll be here," Alix says, holding her look.

Trissa suddenly looks at me through narrowed eyes.

Ack! Does she know?

I hustle away, as if disappearing will put an end to Trissa's suspicions. On my way, I notice with surprise that it looks like *everybody* is at this dance. Maybe because seventh grade is when we get our first real dance. I guess I didn't see it as that big of a deal. But it clearly is for most people.

I'm not surprised to see Alicia Alongi, Emma Cruz, and Brie Collins standing by the wall. They're probably making fun of people, as per usual. Johnny Granday, one of the school's main bullies (and one of my prime suspects in the Ella Baker Shade case) is air-kicking the decorations and laughing with his buddies. I even see Ethan Navarez glowering at a side table and scrawling in a notebook. Which I guess I shouldn't judge him for, with my pile of notebooks and all. Even though I highly dislike all of these people, it makes me feel nostalgic for my last mystery. It seems so long ago now.

When I get to the hallway, I note that the coat check isn't far from the girls' bathroom. This isn't ideal, with Mr. Crohner manning the post, but hopefully it won't cause a problem.

As I approach the coat check, I spot Connor and Brian. "Hey!" I greet them.

"Check out Drew wearing a dress!" Connor says, his eyes popping. "I didn't think I'd ever see you out of a pair of sweats."

I frown nervously. "Why, is it bad?"

"No!" Brian says, elbowing his date. "Connor only meant you look good. Right?"

Connor nods, giving me a faux-exasperated look as he hands over a jacket to Mr. Crohner. He looks at Brian expectantly.

"Nuh-uh," Brian says, smoothing the lines on his velvety blazer. "And get this stolen too? I don't think so."

"That *is* a cool jacket," I say.

There are a lot of nice things on the racks and shelves behind Mr. Crohner, actually. Nice-looking coats and purses line the back area. Possibly a *thief's* wonderland. Not only is my jacket nice, but I'm also pretty sure that French Connection is a good brand for clothes. Possibly an *exclusive* brand.

On impulse, I remove one of the backup glitter bombs from my messenger bag and surreptitiously slip it into my coat before I hand it over. Mr. Crohner smiles and hands me a ticket that reads: *28.*

It couldn't hurt to set a trap in case the whole ransom-note thing is a distraction. Besides, Lita says that a detective has to trust their instincts.

"And *that's* a nice jacket," Brian says to me, looking after it. He frowns. "Are you sure you want to take the risk?"

I think about Mom's text to Mr. Clark. "It doesn't have sentimental value," I say quickly. "Besides, let's just say I have something in the works that could end these thefts *tonight*. Maybe I could even get your Jordans back."

Without hesitation, Brian leans in and gives me a hug that makes me cry out in surprise.

"Oof," I say. "Hey, don't thank me yet."

Connor smiles at both of us, and then looks behind me. "So, are you solving crimes with a . . . date tonight?"

Blushing, I reply, "No date. I'm here with Trissa, Shrey, and his date, Zora. Oh, and . . . umm, Alix Chang?"

"Is that a question?" Connor laughs, but thankfully doesn't notice my awkwardness. Maybe this crush isn't written all over my face like I think it is. Once I say goodbye and promise to give Connor and Brian an update later, I check the time.

Six fifteen.

I head back to find Alix and Trissa and say, "Time to be on watch."

Trissa cranes her neck. "I don't see Olivia yet."

Frowning, Alix looks around. "Kenzie and Sarina are

over there. Maybe she's in the bathroom?"

I peer at Kenzie and Sarina, who are both wearing dresses that look way too expensive for a school dance. Kenzie's hair has a peacock-feather fascinator that matches her blue dress, and Sarina wears a shiny multicolored dress with a series of oddly-matched jewelry—bright-colored gems and silver mixed with gold.

"Didn't Zora's note say that one of the stalls would be out of order?" Trissa asks thoughtfully. "Do you think she got here early? Or would she risk Zora finding her putting up the sign? *She* doesn't know that our plan is to drop the money close to seven."

I bite my lip. As I look at Kenzie and Sarina, where our suspect *should* be, something feels like it's struggling to click into place in my mind. "Probably not, but let me check. Can you two take your stations? Alix, stand a little closer to Kenzie and Sarina—just in case."

They both nod and I dart for the hallway door to head for the bathroom. It does seem unlikely that Olivia would be unprepared enough to put the sign up this late. She's on the dance committee, same as Kenzie.

I walk into the bathroom, and a laminated Out of Order sign is on the far stall, as the note said it would be. But no sign of Olivia. Hastily, I stalk back into the

235

multipurpose room and walk over to my assigned post—just in time to see Zora and Shrey walk in.

Shrey is wearing his usual "nice clothes" that he typically saves for a trip to see his dadi; Shrey's grandmother likes him clean-cut. Still, he looks more than presentable in a pair of ironed olive khaki pants and a black sweater.

Zora looks amazing in a green wrap dress with a sunbeam fascinator. They walk in holding hands, and Zora beams up at Shrey as they cross the landing.

Wow. Holding hands? This is really getting to be a thing.

A few students walk in front of me and, for a moment, I get lost in the shuffle. I try to crane my neck over the heads in the now-busy auditorium. Unfortunately, I'm medium-short, so this doesn't work. Regardless, I manage to spot my friends again. Shrey and Zora are happily chatting with Alix, while Trissa motions for me to join her on the other side of the room.

"Hey!" Trissa says, a little too loudly even over the music. "Did you see anything?"

I lean in closer to her. "Not really," I say, frustration creeping into my voice. "I saw the Out of Order sign. But no Olivia."

If Olivia is planning on getting her money from Zora

tonight, wouldn't she have her eyes on Zora? "Maybe we should—" I'm about to tell Trissa we should find them, when something makes me stop.

Olivia Campos might not be death-staring Zora and Shrey right now, but someone is:

Preethi Agarwal.

24

"DID YOU SEE THAT LOOK?" Trissa asks. She's staring at Preethi, too.

"Sure did," I mutter. "It doesn't exactly prove she's a thief, but she looks upset to see him and Zora. Maybe Shrey was right and she's involved somehow? We should talk to her at least."

"Did you just say 'Shrey was right'?" Trissa asks.

"I said he was *maybe* right, and I'll deny it if you even tell him that," I say quickly.

Trissa giggles in reply as we make our way through a group of students. By the time we get over to where Preethi is standing, her expression has returned to normal. Now, she merely leans on her right forearm crutch, laughing with her friend Sofia.

"Hi, Preethi," I greet her.

"Hey!" she says, blinking at Trissa and me with

surprise. "What's up? Did you find my Magicase?"

"We haven't found anything . . . yet," Trissa says carefully. She gestures to Preethi's outfit. "Cool dress, by the way. Did you decorate your crutches to match?"

Preethi waves the hand she's not using up and down her sparkly champagne-colored dress. "Bling all over, right?"

I look appreciatively at the complementary glitter-style tape wrapped around her crutches like candy-cane stripes. "Very cool," I agree. "Um, can we talk to you for a second?"

Preethi furrows her brow. "Sure."

Sofia doesn't make a move to leave, so I decide to launch right into Lita's first interrogation technique: think fast.

"Did you steal Zora's bracelet and send her creepy notes to get back at Shrey?" I say, before I can talk myself out of it.

Preethi, Sofia, and Trissa all look a bit shocked. Trissa gives me a look that says: *That escalated quickly.* I shrug at her, trying to convey in my look that I know what I'm doing. Specifically, Lita Miyamoto's interrogation technique #1.

"What are you talking about?" Preethi asks, her surprised expression quickly turning into one of offense.

"We just saw you looking over at Zora and Shrey,"

Trissa says, looking to me for affirmation. When I nod, she goes on. "You looked mad."

"And?" Sofia cuts in. "She has every right to be mad!"

"Sofia! God!" Preethi wails, looking mortified.

Sofia crosses her arms. "Well, it's true. After you wrote him that note, he just crumpled it up and threw it away. I mean, did he expect you to be friendly after that?"

"So, you are writing notes," I say.

"Yes. I mean, no!" Preethi cries. "I didn't write creepy notes to you, okay? I promise. I knew Shrey liked you, but I didn't blame you or anything."

For a moment, I don't know what she's talking about. Then, I remember that I'd told her *I* was receiving the notes—not Zora. But, what does that have to do with the fact that Shrey used to like me?

Trissa blinks at Sofia and Preethi, and I can tell that her mind is moving a mile a minute like mine. After a second, a look of realization crosses her face. "You wrote Shrey a note telling him that you like him."

Preethi slumps over, looking humiliated. "Liked!" she moans. "Past tense, okay? LIKED."

Whoa.

Scanning my memory for what she said before, I say, "And he threw the note away."

"Yup," Sofia says, scowling. "He took the note out of his backpack and then *spit* in it and threw it away."

"That doesn't sound like something Shrey would do," I say.

"Yeah, well he did," Preethi says, laughing humorlessly. "But I don't even care. He obviously likes Zora now and I've moved on."

Trissa gives me a knowing look. "Okay, Preethi," she says. "So, you're sure you didn't write any notes or take anything from the PE lockers?"

"No way," she says. "I would never steal."

"Maybe Shrey is the one you should be talking to," Sofia says harshly. Then, she motions for Preethi to stand up and follow her. The two girls give us one last look before they disappear into the crowd.

"Well, that was weird," Trissa says.

"It was," I reply. "But I didn't get the sense they were lying. And that sure as heck would explain why she's been eye-stabbing Shrey recently." As soon as I say the last part, I realize I haven't been looking out for my prime suspect. "Wait. We need to find Olivia."

Trissa points toward the stage, where Olivia is talking to Ms. Tuitasi by the speakers. "I've got eyes on her now," she says.

I grin at Trissa. "I can't believe you're so good at this

when you never watch true crime."

She shrugs. "My parents and I like baking competitions. Besides, I like to be part of the action, not watch it on a screen."

"Unless it's epic wars in a galaxy far, far away," I point out.

Trissa touches her nose, indicating that I'm right.

"It's already six thirty," Shrey says nervously as soon as we approach. He and Zora are already standing with Alix near the exit. "What was up with Preethi?" he asks.

"More on that later," I tell him, shooting a meaningful look at Trissa. I don't want to distract Shrey with the Preethi angle until we're past this drop. "We thought we had a lead, but it went cold. Cold as ice." Shrey opens his mouth, but I put a hand up. "And don't tell me I'm talking like an old British detective again. I know."

"Rescinded," he says. "So, Trissa and I are going to keep watch here, right?"

"While we go to the bathroom," Zora says, eying Alix and me nervously.

I nod. I'm about to reply when a new song comes on. The frenetic and loud beat drowns out my voice as I try to shout instructions. "Trissa, you watch the entrance! Shrey, you'll want to see if you can keep eyes on Olivia! You need a bird's-eye view!"

"FEED A HERD OF WHAT?" Shrey yells over the music.

Even after guiding the group to the hallway entrance, the music is too loud to be heard without giving away our whole plan. I motion for them to follow me into the hallway, past the coat check where it's a bit quieter. "You take the bleachers," I tell Shrey. "So you can see better."

He nods. "Got it."

Trissa rocks back and forth on her heels excitedly. "So. Are we doing this?"

Alix grins, tugging on the lapels of her leather jacket. "It's go time."

I slip Zora the envelope, containing the card, the money, and the glitter bomb. She takes it, and looks nervously at Shrey.

"It's okay," he says, smiling down at her. "Worst-case scenario, we can still just go talk to Ms. El-Sayed or Mr. Lopez."

Zora nods, still looking shaken. "Okay."

"And we'll be there, in case anyone tries to corner you," Alix assures her.

I look up at the clock in the auditorium, which now reads 6:38. "We'd better go," I say. "Give Alix and me a few minutes to get in position. We'll be watching."

Alix winks at me and the flutter is back big-time. "I'd hate to be on your bad side, Leclair," she says.

"You have *no* idea," Shrey says.

Trissa and Shrey move back into the auditorium to take their places, while Zora hangs near the coat check. It's only thirty seconds before I get a text.

Jedi Detective Agency MMS; Me, Trissa Jacobs, and 1 other

> **TRISSA:** Olivia is dancing by the speakers. Will update.

I frown as Alix and I walk down the hall. "Olivia doesn't exactly look like she's preparing to collect a ransom."

"Do you think something's up?" she asks.

Looking over my shoulder, I frown. "I figured Olivia would be the one disappearing by now. And Kenzie and Sarina are nowhere to be found. Are they still outside?"

"Didn't we clear them?" Alix asks.

"I don't know," I murmur in reply. "Something is off."

We walk into the bathroom and stuff ourselves into the first stall. Fortunately, there's a tile ledge at the rear wall of all the stalls, so Alix and I don't have to crowd together on a toilet.

Still, now that I'm considering it, crowding together with Alix doesn't sound that bad. Except the toilet part. Of course, merely thinking this makes me want to facepalm. What *is* this?

Alix locks the stall door behind us and hoists herself up on the shallow ledge. I follow suit, sitting next to her.

"So, Leclair. Is this, like, a regular thing for you?"

"These days. Well, usually not in bathrooms."

"Any pointers?" he asks. "This is my first sting operation, boss." She says the last part like an old-timey mobster. "Don't want to end up sleeping with the fishes after this." She laughs and wags a finger by her face. I watch the charms on her bracelet, momentarily hypnotized.

OBSERVATIONS:

• A funny feeling takes over me again, and this time it has nothing to do with the hormone cult.
• I can't stop staring at her bracelet and the deep red crescent moon charm.

CONCLUSIONS: WAIT . . .

"Your bracelet," I say, instinctively reaching for it.

Alix offers me her wrist. "What is it?"

My mind is racing so fast, I have to try to slow it down before I can speak. "Something bothered me about your and Zora's matching charms, but I couldn't put a finger on it. Now I remember. I've seen it somewhere else."

"Where?" Trissa asks.

"*Sarina*," I say hurriedly. "She's wearing an almost identical bracelet. Well, hers is a little different, but it's the same *charms*. A heart and a crescent moon. Both with dark red stones."

"Zora loves garnet," Alix says, her eyes widening.

"Yes. Zora says she likes to make her own charms for people. Like her *best friends*. Sarina was Zora's best friend in the Kenzie group, right?"

"Yes," Alix confirms. "But didn't we clear Sarina of the thefts? I thought she was on a vacation with her family thousands of miles away."

"Sarina didn't steal anything from Preethi and Jazz," I mutter. "And not Juan, either. His theft was the first week back from break."

My eyes feel like they're moving as fast as my brain, recalling each moment I'd come face-to-face with the Kenzie crew. During dance prep, at the spa. And, in Sarina's case, in the *library*.

We'd eliminated Sarina for the early thefts, but not Kenzie or Olivia. And then we'd ruled out Kenzie for the ransom notes because she didn't have the means to leave the notes. Trissa wasn't wrong about the thefts having to be connected. But maybe we're looking at something a lot more complicated than I thought . . .

"Drew," Alix says, seeing my face. "What is it?"

"It never made sense that Zora was the only one to get a ransom notes early on," I ramble. I can practically feel my eyes bugging out. "Writing notes is something personal . . ." I trail off, thinking of the letter that Lita Miyamoto wrote to the Masterpiece Man before she caught him, and the letter I'd tried to write to my mom.

"Sarina has been wearing that charm bracelet every day I've seen her. Even poolside at the Clearview Spa. Why would she still be wearing Zora's friendship charm if they haven't spoken in the better part of a year?"

"Wait, so you think she wrote the ransom notes," Alix says, knitting her brow. "Does that mean she didn't steal anything at all?"

Setting my jaw, I say, "I think we're looking at a copycat within the crime. The two thefts with notes— my pen and Zora's bracelet, have the same modus operandi."

"MO." Alix nods. "Got it."

I can't help but smile. "Anyway, the thief dumped other items of value back in the lockers. That did prove that the thefts were connected. But what if they *are* connected, only not the way we think? What if all three girls are involved and Sarina did the ransom notes and two of the thefts on the side? Zora's bracelet, and my pen as a warning?"

Alix's jaw drops. "If Sarina is on the inside, she would know exactly how to match the thefts to the real perpetrator. That means—"

Both of us freeze and snap our mouths shut as the door swings open.

We let a breath out when we hear Zora humming the *Simpsons* theme (our agreed-upon code song). Still, we stay quiet in case anyone is following behind. After a few seconds, we hear the door to the far stall slam shut. Then, we hear Zora exit and the bathroom door swing closed.

"That means," Alix repeats in a whisper, "that Sarina could have used the thefts to mess with Zora. Then later, to threaten you to stay off the case."

"Possibly," I say solemnly, matching her tone. "But there's something else. Olivia might be getting the lock combinations, but I think Kenzie might be the real thief."

"Why? She's so rich she could afford any of that stuff," Alex hisses.

"I think it's a lot like the Masterpiece Man," I murmur, breaking off with a blush when I realize what I've said. "Um, you see, there's this art thief . . ."

"The Masterpiece Man. Stole art along the Eastern Seaboard for, like, ten years," Alix says. "Please, Leclair. I told you; I podcast."

"Wait, are you listening to *Game Over* right now?" I ask, jaw dropped.

"Omigod, *yes*. I love it," Alix says. Then she breaks off and stares at me. "Wait! Your pen. You said that Lita Miyamoto gave it to you, but you never explained the inscription. Were those the words from Dr. Miyamoto's note to the Masterpiece Man? Gerald and Max played it last week . . ."

"Yes!" I say a little too loudly.

I clamp my mouth shut. For half a second, I swear I must be blushing so hard that I might turn into a tomato and roll away. "Anyhow," I go on, "if you know the Masterpiece Man, then you might know that he didn't even resell the art. He was rich himself. He only took art because he believed others didn't deserve it. Although, I don't think they've gotten there in the podcast yet."

"Whoa. That could be Kenzie. She's . . . controlling."

I smile shyly. "Anyway, it's just a theory."

Alix puts a hand on mine and three things happen, in rapid succession:

1. My stomach flips so hard I think I might die.
2. I realize that, other than the "I might die" part, this . . . isn't so bad.
3. The bathroom door swings open.

Both of us freeze again, watching the footsteps under the door. A long *creak* sounds when the last stall opens. Then the sound of paper ripping.

Then, a bloodcurdling scream.

25

ALIX AND I JUMP DOWN in unison when the scream sounds. However, by the time we open the stall door, all we see is a flash of black hair exiting through the door, and a trail of glitter on the ground.

When we walk outside, there's Sarina Masoumi— her arms and hands sparkling with various shades of glitter. She's facing off with Zora in the hallway, with a look of intense hatred blazing in her eyes.

"What . . . *is* this?" Sarina hisses at Zora. "Did *you* do this?"

Nervously, I look down the hallway. Surely *someone* must have heard that scream. But, then I hear the loud beat pulsating from the entrance suddenly die down. The music must have drowned it out, because not even Mr. Crohner is looking our way. Not yet, at least.

"Did you just try to collect *ransom* money in the bathroom?" Alix counters Sarina's question, crossing her arms. "After stealing Zora's bracelet?"

Sarina looks back at us, alarmed. She clearly thought she was only dealing with Zora.

"Why did you write the ransom notes, Sarina?" I ask bluntly. Depending on how loud this is about to get, we don't have much time before someone notices a girl who looks like she dunked both arms in a barrel full of glitter.

Sarina sets her jaw, remaining stubbornly silent.

"You really scared me!" Zora cries indignantly. "I mean, we used to be *friends*."

The word sets a fire in Sarina's eyes. "*Friends?* Really? After you abandoned me?" She spits each word out like it tastes bad and Alix moves forward.

"Now wait a second," she says, holding up her hands. "You can't talk to Zora that way."

"I can't? Says who? *She's* the one who left me behind. I have every right to be angry." Sarina brushes a strand of black hair out of her eyes, but it only streaks her face and hair with flour and glitter.

"So you came up with a plan to scare Zora with the notes," I prompt her.

"What are you even *doing* here, anyway?" Sarina asks me. "I thought I told you to back off. You're always

252

snooping around in everyone's business." She rubs furiously at her arm.

I'm trying to keep my voice as calm as possible, like Lita would do during a standoff. "I'm here to help my friend. And get my stuff back, thank you very much."

Sarina blinks at me, confused. "Wait. What stuff?"

"My *pen*?" I remind her flatly. "As in, the one you stole before you wrote me that note."

Sarina's voice is dripping with disdain as she says, "Why would I steal a *pen*?" I check her face for the usual signs of lying, but . . . nothing.

Alix rounds on Sarina. "Whatever. You're clearly lying, Sarina. You sent Drew that note."

"Yeah, but—" Sarina starts to protest.

Alix ignores her, going on. "And Zora didn't *abandon* you. She tried to keep talking to you after she and I became friends. You didn't want anything to do with her."

"I didn't then and I don't now," Sarina says through clenched teeth.

"Then why are you wearing that bracelet?" I counter. "If you don't care, why wouldn't you have thrown away the friendship bracelet that Zora made for you?"

I see Zora's gaze flit down toward Sarina's wrist and her eyes widen with understanding.

"And if you do care," Zora adds, "why would you do this to me?"

"I only—"

Zora cuts her off. "You took my bracelet and left me notes in the library saying you were *watching* me. Then, when I tried to get help from Drew, you threatened *her*! Don't you get how messed up that is?"

Sarina looks between Alix and Zora. "Clearly, none of you can take a joke. Which is funny, considering you pranked *me* with glitter and fake money."

"A joke," Zora repeats sadly. "So, this whole thing was a joke. Stealing from me and Drew, the notes—not to mention stealing from everyone else?"

Sarina casts a nervous look behind us. "I don't know what you're talking about."

"You didn't steal from the others," I say flatly.

Sarina reddens. "Well, I definitely didn't take some boring pen. I took a twenty out of your bag. Big deal."

A twenty? Does she mean the money that Dad gave me for the ink? Her words catch me off guard for a moment, but I push ahead. "I mean the *other* thefts," I say firmly. "The ones that gave you the idea. You and Olivia helped, but Kenzie is the one who stole everything else. Wasn't she?"

Sarina still presses her mouth shut, refusing to speak.

"All right, fine," I say, "I guess we'd better go find Mr. Lopez . . ."

Sarina holds out a glitter-coated hand. "Wait. Don't do that." She digs around in her clutch purse until she retrieves a bracelet that looks identical to Alix's.

"Here," she yells, tossing it on the floor in front of us.

The bracelet, along with the card filled with money-shaped paper scraps, and one twenty-dollar bill lie scattered on the floor in front of us. But not my Lita pen. Could she actually be telling the truth?

My eyes move to the entrance, where a few students are finally noticing us. I'm not surprised. Sarina is getting louder, and it sounds like they're playing a quieter slow song. Mr. Crohner pops his head out of the coat check, tossing looks of concern in our direction.

"So. You have your stuff back," Sarina goes on. "That's what matters to you, right?"

"It's not all that matters to *me*," Zora says. "I still want to know why you did this."

"Because you left me alone with THEM, okay?!" Sarina says, raising her voice again. "Kenzie and Olivia are the *worst*. Especially Kenzie."

"Then why are you friends with them?" Zora asks. "I know they're the worst. That's why I had to leave! And I tried to reach out to you after that joke you played on

Alix, but you wouldn't talk to me."

"It was so easy for you to replace me, wasn't it?" Sarina wails.

Zora scrunches her face, tears starting to stream down her cheek. "It wasn't you anymore, Sarina. I wasn't replacing you. You weren't the same friend I knew."

Out of the corner of my eye, I see Trissa walk through the hallway door, frantically motioning. Shrey isn't far behind, and then another familiar face follows. *Vice Principal Lopez.* I gulp, watching as he motions to Mr. Crohner to follow him. They're still a hallway's length away. I try not to show my nerves as I stay quiet, watching as Zora and Sarina hash it out.

"If Kenzie is so awful, why didn't you leave *with* me?" Zora cries.

"Because nobody says no to Kenzie Perl!" Sarina shouts. "She has to have *everything.* It's not enough that her family has, like, a mansion. It's not enough that she has free access to the Clearview Spa every week. When she wants something, she takes it. As far as she's concerned, it's already hers!"

My nerves ratchet up as Shrey and Trissa get closer, Vice Principal Lopez trailing behind. "Tell us who stole from the other students, Sarina," I press.

"It was all Kenzie!" Sarina shrieks. "I knew she was

stealing and I knew how. Olivia gave her the locker combinations, but I swear, Kenzie made us stay quiet. I might have taken the bracelet and written those notes, but she's the one who's been stealing. She takes *everything*." Sarina rounds back on Zora. "You were supposed to protect me from her. I couldn't get out."

"I'm sorry, Sarina," Zora says tearfully. "I tried—I really did."

"You don't need to apologize to h—" Alix cuts herself off, her eyes widening as she sees Mr. Lopez come to a stop behind us.

"Girls," he says. "Let's calm down and head to my office."

We all slump down, moving to follow the vice principal, when another sound rips through the hallway.

"AAAUUUUUGHH!"

The high-pitched wail comes from the coat check area and, this time, everyone hears.

We all swivel around to find Kenzie Perl.

26

KENZIE EMERGES FROM THE RACKS of coats at the other end of the hallway. Her dress, as well as her arms and chest, are covered in glitter.

I suppress a smile. Looks like that second trap paid off after all.

RIP my leather jacket, though.

Kenzie's eyes are murderous as she turns to glare at Sarina. "Did you do this?" she yells.

"Now, wait a minute, girls," Mr. Crohner says.

"You and Olivia are the only two people who knew!" Kenzie keeps yelling, advancing toward Sarina. She doesn't even seem to register that any of the rest of us are there, let alone Mr. Lopez.

"It was them," Sarina protests, pointing at us. "They set some kind of trap. I swear, I didn't tell them you were the one stealing."

Kenzie lunges for Sarina, but Vice Principal Lopez calmly steps between them, closing his eyes as if gathering his patience.

"So," he says. "We have stolen property, a public confession from the locker thief, and what appears to be . . . glitter traps?" His eyes open and then glide over, resting squarely on me. "Why am I not surprised that this has something to do with *you*?"

I look at the vice principal sheepishly. "But I'm almost positive I didn't break any school rules this time," I tell him. "I checked the student handbook and everything!"

In spite of himself, he smiles as he shakes his head. "Regardless, I think you all need to come with me to the office."

"The office?" I repeat, my stomach sinking as I think about the Plan and imagine another ding on my record.

Mr. Lopez seems to notice my expression. "We just need to get everything straightened out. I have a feeling you and your friends might have some information for me." Then he mutters, "As per usual."

I nod, falling into step with Shrey and Trissa as we walk down the hall. For a moment, with all the kids staring at us, I feel like we're being perp-walked or something. But, after Vice Principal Lopez motions for Olivia to follow, Alix pokes me from behind.

"Look up, Leclair," she whispers.

I force myself to look up, and *whoa*. All the eyes in the gym are trained on Olivia, Sarina, and Kenzie. However many students overheard that hallway confession, I'll bet it's spreading like wildfire now.

The richest girl in school is the one terrorizing the students by stealing their prized possessions. It actually sounds like something out of a podcast. Our very own *Game Over*.

"Wait here, please," the vice principal instructs as he gets on the walkie. "Hey, Chris. Can you also grab Brian Wu, Preethi Agarwal, and Liz Davis?"

"Um, also Juan Madrigal, Emma Cruz, and Jazz Aguilar," I tell him. Then I redden as I see Kenzie, Sarina, and Olivia's matching death glares. "Um, they were . . . also victims of the thefts."

Vice Principal Lopez grins openly at me this time, barking the other names into his walkie. Then he says, "Zora and Sarina, I'd like to talk to you two first."

Principal El-Sayed breezes through the door at that moment, her own walkie-talkie chirping with overlapping voices. "Mr. Crohner will gather up the rest of them," she tells the vice principal. Then she looks at us. "Olivia, why don't you come with me. Kenzie, I'll be out for you in a moment."

Olivia presses her mouth into a thin line, looking irritably back at Kenzie.

Then, the vice principal motions Zora and Sarina into his office and moves to close the door behind them. Which, of course, leaves me, Shrey, Trissa, and Alix with Kenzie. With only a solitary security guard standing watch.

Yikes.

At least we outnumber her.

"I can't believe you narced on us," Kenzie snipes as soon as the door closed.

Hmmm. I guess they all use that word. Which makes sense. I read this anthropology article once about how dialects develop in language and—

"You all are *literally* the worst," Kenzie goes on.

"Really?" Shrey says. "We're the worst? You're the one who's been stealing."

"When you clearly don't need to," Alix pipes in with a snort.

"None of those kids needed that stuff," Kenzie says with an eye-roll.

"And you do?" Alix counters.

"They wouldn't know how to use it right," Kenzie says, her voice dripping with disdain.

"Whatever," Trissa says, glaring at her. "Liz knows

how to use a Harper Berry better than you. Clearly." She gestures to Kenzie's bright eye makeup.

"Excuse me?" Kenzie snaps. She moves forward, and the security guard steps forward as if on cue. "Sit back, miss," the woman says curtly. Kenzie crosses her arms petulantly, but complies.

"Even after this, everyone is going to love me and hate you," Kenzie says. "You know why?"

Alix rolls her eyes. "Illuminate us."

"Because I have something they need. My dad pays for all the good events at this school. You think the district is making that happen? No. It's me. *My* family. And you all are just a bunch of snitches. People *hate* snitches."

I'd been sitting quietly through the commotion, but a swell of anger courses through me. All this time, I assumed Kenzie was like the Masterpiece Man. Someone who has their own twisted set of principles. But it was still principles. From how Kenzie was talking, it sounded like this was a lot more about controlling people. Taking things so that she could give them and seem all benevolent. Keeping people in line so they would *need* her. All of a sudden, I can't stay quiet another second.

"I wouldn't be so sure about that, Kenzie," I say,

trying to keep my voice even.

"Sure about what?" she spits.

"That everyone will love you after this. Did you see everyone's faces when we walked out? They don't care that your dad paid for this dance," I say flatly. "All the kids you stole from *definitely* don't. And they have friends. Their friends have friends."

"Oh, what—" Kenzie begins, but I cut her off. I'm on a roll now.

"You made everyone at this school scared," I go on. "Which was the point, I guess. But, here's the thing. For most kids who don't live in a huge mansion, that stuff wasn't just expensive. It was *important*. They had to work for it, unlike you. Do you really think the people you terrorized are going to love you tomorrow after you made them afraid to bring their stuff to school? I don't think so. But, hey, what do I know? I'm just a snitch. Right?"

"You're nobody," Kenzie says, but her voice falters.

"We're the ones who caught you," Trissa says, motioning to me, Shrey, and Alix. "Us."

Kenzie opens her mouth to retort but the door to Vice Principal Lopez's office opens, startling us all. "Kenzie," he says gruffly. "You're up next."

A smile spreads across my face. Trissa's words

immediately bring to mind Lita's famous call-out to the Masterpiece Man.

"It will be me."

We may only be in seventh grade. And these thefts might not be the crime of the century. But, still. It makes me wonder what Lita Miyamoto could do if she had friends like mine.

27

"GLITTER BOMBS?" DAD IS REPEATING incredulously. "*Glitter* bombs."

He came to pick me up, but we're still sitting in the
Ella Baker Middle School parking lot. So we can "talk,"
Dad says.

"Okay," I protest. "But hear me out! It wasn't the
kind where anything actually *explodes* at you. I mean,
kids pull this on each other at school all the time—"

"Which is the only reason you're not in trouble," Dad
cuts me off. "Mr. Lopez said that you should have come
to him before setting a trap, and I agree with him."

"I should have. I guess I wanted to figure it out
myself," I mumble, looking down. "But that's no excuse."
I almost add another confession—that part of me needed
that dance showdown because I wanted to spend more

time with Alix. But the thought of saying it out loud is too mortifying for me to bear.

Dad smiles, but it's a sad smile. "Drew. I'm just going to ask you something, okay?"

"Okaaay," I drawl, wincing.

He cleans his glasses and doesn't even care that I see. *Oof.*

"Dad. Just say it."

He rests a hand on my shoulder. "This visit from your mom is hitting you harder than I thought, isn't it?"

The question hits me in the gut. Truthfully, with the whole Kenzie and company takedown, I'd finally almost forgotten about Mom, and that text to Mr. Clark. It had been nice to forget about it for a little while.

I let out a whimper when it comes flooding back over me, and then the tears come. Dad puts his arms around me, holding me tight. I let out a little muffled sob, and then I spill about what happened with Mom— everything from overhearing the thing she said about me solving mysteries, to our odd conversation about liking boys and girls the night before, to the Mr. Clark text. "I thought she was here to see me. She *said* she was," I whisper. More annoying tears come, but I'm able to calm them down quickly.

"Oh, bun. I'm so sorry," Dad says, wrapping me tight

and cradling my head with his hand. "But I promise—your mom *is* here to see you."

I pull up my skirt to wipe my nose. "Then why did she say that to Mr. Clark?"

Dad takes a long breath in preparation, like he's trying to figure out how to frame it. "Drew, your mom is so . . . vibrant and fun. She's a good person at heart. But I think she tries to be a different version of herself for different people."

I scoff. "Why would a person do that? That doesn't make any sense."

"Because you won't be anyone but yourself. You're different." Dad wipes a stray tear on my cheek and smiles. "It's hard to explain. I told you a little bit about your grandpa Roy and how Mom had a hard time growing up. She had to pretend to be this perfect little girl to get his affection."

"That sounds familiar," I say bitterly. "I had to try to pretend to be a normal kid for her to pay any attention to me."

"Sometimes we're doomed to make the same mistakes our parents made," he says. "I know it's hard to understand. And we *are* moving the divorce faster than I thought we would. But, Drew . . . your mom is ecstatic to see you. Between our fights this week, the only thing we can agree on is how great you are."

"Oh, come on," I scoff.

"It's true," he promises. "She's had such a good time with you this week. Drew, she's already planned out her next trip, including everything you'll do together."

I break free of his embrace and look up at him, blinking. "Really?"

"Yep. She's coming back in April and staying with Wendy so that she can make it a longer trip. She says she wants to really talk about your plans for the future, and how she can help with Grandpa Roy's trust. But it's not all about money. I think she wants to connect with you—to get to know the real you."

I bite my lip and suppress the urge to remind him how familiar this sounds. "But, if she's like a chameleon, how do I know she *really* wants to spend time with me? How do I know that part's real?"

"It's real," he says, in a way that makes me believe him immediately. "I just know."

I settle back into a curled-up position, resting my head in the crook of his shoulder. "Dad?" I ask. "Do *you* think it's a total fantasy that I might be like Lita someday? A criminal profiler, I mean."

"No, I don't," he says. "And I don't think your mom does, either. She was only . . . trying to go about protecting you the wrong way. I'm not excusing it, though. I know it hurt you, and that's what matters."

Squeezing him, I say, "I love you, Dad. Like . . . a *lot*."

"Times a splabillion," he says softy. "Okay. Now, tell me what happens after the glitter-not-technically-bombs."

I bring him up to speed on the rest of the story, and he does seem to be listening intently. When I get to the part about the note I got from Sarina, he gasps. "The *Lita* pen?!" he cries, horrified.

"I know," I say morosely. "And she didn't even admit to it. So, either she's lying, or she's telling the truth and I totally lost it. Like I lose *everything*."

"I'll help you look for the Lita pen, sweetheart," he promises. "That is too precious to stay lost."

"Right?" I say, smiling gratefully. I continue with the whole story, ending when Mr. Lopez found us and my second glitter trap exploded.

"Wow," he says when I take a breath. "Having you as a daughter is sort of like having my very own personal true-crime podcast."

I laugh. "That's . . . probably not a good thing, unless you're you."

"Probably," he says, turning on the car.

When we're on the road, I turn back to Dad

thoughtfully. "When I started looking into this, I thought Kenzie was exactly like the Masterpiece Man," I tell him. "She was even worse, because she was using her money to control people. But she has *everything*. Why isn't that enough for her? Why did she have to take from people?"

"Well, deep down she must be a very sad, very scared person. Especially if she feels like she needs to steal from people to maintain this sense of being above everyone," Dad says. "Also, for some people, even too much is never enough."

"Oooh. That sounds like the tagline of a good crime podcast."

"It really does!" Dad agrees.

When he pulls onto our street, I ask the question I've been dreading for the last hour.

"So, what are the consequences? My punishment, I mean. Mr. Lopez let me off the hook because I was so careful not to break any rules. But I can tell you won't."

Dad pulls into the driveway and tugs up the parking brake before turning to face me. "You're right. I'm glad you told me that you were looking for Zora's bracelet, but I really wish you'd told me the whole story. But, since I haven't been completely forthcoming with you, I feel like a big punishment would be hypocritical. I'm thinking let's make the 'punishment' fit the crime.

So . . . we increase the time on our father-daughter talks to forty-five minutes. More chances for these little lies of omission to slip out. Fair?"

"Fair."

"And I think we need to talk about therapy to sort out this Mom stuff."

I knew that the last one was coming. "Okay," I agree.

"Oh, before we go into the house," Dad says. "I should tell you that Mom's here."

"What? Why?" I yelp instinctively.

He leans back in his seat. "We signed the papers tonight, sweetie. It will take another month or two to move forward, but . . . well, there it is."

I struggle to pin down how I'm feeling, but even I'm not quite sure. So, I peer at him and ask, "Are you sad?"

"A little," Dad says. "But I'm also excited in a way. Relationships change, bun. There's no way around it. Sometimes change ends up being the best thing that can happen to you."

Sighing, I lean back too. "It feels like everything is changing so fast, though. Shrey has a girlfriend now. A *girlfriend*."

"I know," Dad says.

"It bothered me, I guess. But not because I'm jealous of Zora. I think I'd feel the same way if Trissa got a boyfriend—" I break off, snorting as I remember a detail from after the big bust. "She might have one soon, who knows? After Vice Principal Lopez talked to all of us, I saw Trissa talking to one of the three boys she doesn't find disgusting."

"That's a ringing endorsement," Dad points out.

"It is for Trissa," I say. "It's this guy Simon Branden. He has a Mandalorian patch on his backpack, and is what Trissa calls 'yummy to look at,' whatever that means."

"You know, they'll probably feel the same way if you start to like someone," Dad says. "But, even if you don't, it doesn't mean you'll get left behind, bun."

I look at him sharply. It's like he actually reached in to look at my soul with that one statement. That *is* what I've been worried about, for so long. With Mom, and now with Shrey. But, things are also different today than they were yesterday.

Swallowing hard, I say, "Um, Dad? What if . . . I *do* like someone?"

He smiles. "Then, I hope they're good enough for you. Whoever they are. Because you're pretty special."

He didn't say "I hope *he's* good enough for you." He didn't ask me if I'm dating Trissa. I feel tears prick at my eyes. "Thanks, Dad. I'm not ready to talk about it quite yet, okay?"

"Okay," Dad says. "But I'm here when you do. And I don't think you need to worry about Shrey. Change might happen faster when you're this age, but the people who are supposed to stay in your life, *stay*."

I look at Dad thoughtfully. "You know, I think that's why Sarina sent Zora the ransom notes. Their relationship changed, and Sarina thought it was Zora who changed. It sounded like she was upset about being left behind too. But why would she stay friends with Kenzie?"

Dad grins. "Well, I think, for that, we have to remember what Lita Miyamoto said."

"About perpetrators and bait?"

"Nope. That some people can't break free of their cycles."

We sit with that for a few minutes, and then Dad reaches for the door handle. "Yeah," I say in response. "We shouldn't leave Mom waiting."

28

WHEN WE GET INSIDE, MOM is pacing worriedly in the living room. "There you are!" she cries, pulling me in for a hug when she sees me. "I was worried! What happened?"

Dad and I look at each other. "Um," he says. "There were some kids stealing at school. Drew and her friends found out who was responsible."

"So, we had to tell the vice principal," I put in.

That sounds almost normal. Right? And it's *mostly* true.

"Is this that mystery you were talking about?"

"Yeah, Mom."

"Oh!" she says. "Was it those mean girls we saw? Tell me everything."

Dad gives me a pointed look. "Hey, I'm going to start

putting away all this paperwork," he says. "Why don't you go chat with your mom before it's bedtime."

Both of us nod, and I gesture for Mom to follow me to my room.

"So, was it? Those girls, I mean?" she asks eagerly.

"It was," I say, suppressing a laugh. It's funny that Mom had zeroed in on all three of them when I had been so sure it was only Olivia. Maybe I didn't just inherit my knack for mystery-solving from Dad.

"So . . ." she begins awkwardly. "I know I'm leaving soon. But I wanted to say I've had so much fun with you. I would really like to come back and visit soon."

A bitter pang twists in my chest. "Are you sure?"

"Of course!"

I suddenly become very interested in my thumbnail. "Okay. I guess I thought you weren't here to see me at all."

Mom's face scrunches in confusion. "What?"

Inhaling a long breath, I brace myself. *Just say this one thing*, I tell myself, *or you'll just be angry again until next time she comes.*

"I thought maybe you were only here to sign the divorce papers so you could get as far away from us as you could," I say, embarrassed when I can't get the words out without crying.

Mom looks stunned for a moment. I can't help but think that, if this were Dad, he would already be across the room hugging me. He would already be telling me that I was wrong, and that everything would be okay. But Mom merely stands there, like a deer in headlights, before she finally reacts.

"Wh-why would you think that?" she asks shakily.

"Because you left. *Left* left. As in, to another state. I know Dad says that relationships change, but they're not supposed to change between a mother and daughter. You're supposed to want to be in the same state as I am."

"I-I'm so sorry, sweetie. The last thing I wanted was to make you feel that way."

I force myself to look right at her. She's crying now, too—so hard that I feel guilty.

"But that's what happened. I *did* feel that way."

She walks tentatively toward me, like I might break if she gets too close. Then, she sits at the edge of my bed and lets out a long sigh.

"Drew, I can't take back what I did. But I do want our relationship to be . . . good."

"I know you do. And this visit has actually mostly been okay. But how can our relationship be good when you don't even live here?"

She wipes a tear with her sleeve. "I wish I could

explain. I think the only way we can have a good relationship is if I'm not here. But that's not about you at all. It's about me. *My* failing. My problems."

"Does it have something to do with Grandpa Roy?" I ask quietly.

She looks at me, surprised, and then laughs humorlessly. "Yes and no. I think part of me needs to heal so that I can be a better parent to you. I have . . . episodes. Sometimes I get so sad that I don't know what I'll do."

"I get panic attacks," I point out. "And I don't, like, run away or anything."

"But my sadness was hurting you," she says. "My self-doubt was being put on you. I could see what it was doing to you. And I can't stop it. It feels like I can't *be* here and not mess you up. That kind of sadness spreads, ruining everything. I already hurt your dad. I couldn't have it ruin you, too."

Sneaking a look at her, I say, "So you left before you could hurt me more?"

"In a way," she says.

I want to say a lot more things. Like how she's acting like leaving was this big sacrifice, when it's really selfish. And how being so far away from me only makes things easier on *her.* But, at this moment, I feel like we've said all that we can say. I don't know that Mom will ever really be able to hear what I want to tell her.

And the last thing I want is to let this turn me into something I'm not. Like Sarina—so bitter that I end up hurting people too.

"I do love you, Mom," I say, leaning into her. "But I'm still mad at you."

Her eyes flash with hurt, but she nods. "That's fair, sweetie. I've got some work to do. I know I haven't been supportive enough."

I bite my lip. "Maybe keep asking me about my mysteries. And about Lita. For a while there this week, I really thought you were starting to get it, you know? That this true-crime stuff is *me*. I heard you telling Dad that it was, like, this childish fantasy."

"Oh, Drew—"

"And I get it. I do," I cut her off. "But you're my mom and I need you to believe in me."

She looks teary. "I hear you. I promise I'll try to do better."

"Thanks, Mom."

"Oh!" she says. "Speaking of Lita Mimato."

"Mom! Miyamoto!"

"Oops. Sorry. Anyhow, I forgot to return this."

My jaw must drop all the way to the ground when

she reaches into her purse and hands me the Lita pen.

"I borrowed it to sign the bill at the spa when their pen was dried up. I'm so sorry—I completely forgot until you reminded me just now."

For a moment, I'm not sure what I feel. Should I be angry that Mom was so clueless that she wouldn't realize how much I was missing that pen? Should I feel silly that I made such a big deal to my friends about it, when Sarina had stolen cash out of my bag and I didn't even notice? However, when I rub my fingers over the inscription on the Lita pen, I surprise myself by bursting out into laughter.

"What is it?" Mom asks, smiling.

"Nothing," I say, cackling. "I thought I lost this forever."

"And that's . . . hilarious?"

"A little, yeah!" I wipe a tear from my eye. "I guess I should be happy I didn't lose it. I'm just happy to have it back. Thanks, Mom."

We sit there giggling for a few minutes, the unsaid things weighing on me a little bit less, until Dad finally comes in. They talk for a few minutes, but the minutes kind of blur until I finally hear the front door close.

"So," he says. "Did you tell her?"

I don't answer, but rush over to give him a huge hug.

"I'm so glad you're my dad," I say, tears streaming down my face and onto my pretty dress.

He squeezes me tight and says, "And I'm so happy you're my daughter."

We stay like that until the weight lifts, and my lungs can fill with air again.

29

"THIS IS THE LIFE," TRISSA says, shoving a huge chunk of croissant into her mouth.

"Not gonna lie," Shrey says. "The supply of baked goods was a factor when I befriended Drew in kindergarten."

"Hey!" I protest, glaring at him from behind my sunglasses. "Don't forget my sparkling personality."

Shrey pretends to look nervous. "Uhh, yeah, that too."

Shrey, Trissa, and I are lounging in my backyard, enjoying a lazy Saturday and celebrating our latest mystery triumph. Zora and Alix are joining us soon, and then Connor is coming a little later for a movie night. But it's nice to have some time with the core gang.

"Are we out of croissants already?" Dad calls from

the patio door. He looks at our table, concerned. "Should I get some more?"

"That was me, Mr. Leclair," Trissa says guiltily, eyeing the empty plate. "I'm sorry."

"Never be sorry for loving carbs," Dad says sagely. "Be right back!"

"So," Shrey says, leaning back in his Adirondack chair. "We solved a mystery *and* I got the girl this time. I can't complain about this turn of events."

I smack him playfully. "Yes, you're a total stud."

"Wait!" Trissa yells, springing up. "Speaking of Shrey being a huge stud—"

"That's me," Shrey interrupts, flexing his bicep.

Trissa rolls her eyes, then looks at me. "In all the mess, we never told him about the *Preethi* thing!"

"What Preethi thing? Did you find out why she hates me?"

"Sort of," I say. "Preethi said she wrote you a note and you threw it away."

He frowns. "What note?"

Trissa purses her lips. "Preethi said she wrote you a note at the beginning of the year. You know—telling you she *liked* you."

"Wait, what?"

"She put it in your backpack," Trissa adds. "She said

you read the note, and then spit in it and threw it away."

Shrey's eyes pop. "Oh, no. I grab loose paper from my backpack sometimes to spit out my gum. Do you think—"

"That you spit your gum into a love letter from Preethi? Yeah, pretty sure you did," I say with a cackle.

Shrey looks up a little wistfully. "Preethi likes me. You know, she *is* pretty cute."

"SHREY!" Trissa and I shout in unison.

"What?"

"Um, *Zora*, you out-of-control hormone monster!" I say, swatting him.

Shrey laughs. "I'm not saying I want to go out with her *now*. It's flattering, that's all."

"All right," Trissa says, shaking her head. "I guess we'll give you a pass."

"Do you think I should talk to her?" he asks. When he sees both me and Trissa cross our arms in unison, he adds, "Not like in a romantic way! Just to apologize, and explain about the note?"

"That *would* be nice," Trissa said, cocking her head. "Look at you, being a decent guy about it."

Shrey grins. "Thanks. And, you both like Zora, right?"

"We are both pro-Shrora," I say, exchanging a smile with Trissa.

283

"Wait, *Shrora*? I did not endorse this!" Shrey cries.

"Trissa, want to carry out these plates for me, since they're clearly for you?" Dad calls.

Trissa licks her lips. "Be right back."

"So, you really do like Zora, right?" Shrey asks when we're alone.

"I do."

"And you know . . . I'm not going anywhere. Not bailing. Like, ever. You won't be able to get rid of me, actually."

I smile gratefully at Shrey. "I know."

A silence follows, and I bite my lip. Shrey is my best friend. I *should* tell him about these Cirque-du-Soleil-stomach feelings I'm having about Alix, right? Now that he's not interested in me, he would totally understand . . .

"You know, I just realized I haven't asked you about your mom this whole week," Shrey says before I can open my mouth. He leans toward me and frowns. "Some friend I am."

"It's okay. She left yesterday," I say with a shrug.

"No," he says. "I've been a total dud. Like, I *knew* that this would be a weird week with your mom hanging around, and I basically begged you to talk to me about it. And then I don't even ask you how the visit is going."

"I'll tell you what. Why don't you stay over, like old

times? We can make a fort in the living room and we can talk about it then."

Shrey grins in reply.

"Behold!" Trissa proclaims theatrically, placing two new plates down. "All hail the arrival of the croissants." Trissa *really* loves carbs.

Giggling, I tear off a piece. "So, what do you think the terrible three are doing right about now?" I ask my friends. I drink a sip of my chocolate milk and the straw makes a loud slurping noise.

Shrey snorts. "They're probably back at the Clearview Spa getting manicures."

Trissa leans back. "I don't know. Maybe Sarina and Olivia will finally get away from Kenzie. Now that it's obvious how toxic she is. Besides, Kenzie might not be persona non grata at the spa, but she is at school. For a few days, anyway."

"People have trouble breaking out of their cycles, though," I say, echoing the Lita quotation Dad had said the other night.

Ding-dong!

The doorbell sounds muffled, but we can still hear it float through the patio doors.

"That would be Zora and Alix," Shrey says. He winks, and jogs off.

"What a gentleman," Trissa marvels. She tips her glasses down to peer at me. "So, are you still going to make fun of me for all my shipping? Because Shrora seems pretty solid."

"Shrora forever!" I giggle and clink my chocolate milk glass against hers. "Although, I might need to ship you and Simon Branden now. Were you talking to him *again* yesterday at lunch?"

"He has several fan theories about *Mandalorian*," Trissa says dreamily.

I smirk at her. "Any good ones?"

"We talked about how we both suspect that Baby Yoda is a Sith Lord. It was pretty much a date," she says. "Well, as close to a date as I'm seeing anytime soon, since my dad says no dating until I'm at least fifteen. And then he and Mom are coming with me."

"Yikes, really?" I say.

Trissa nods morosely.

I peer over at the doors, straining to hear the voices inside. Trissa looks over too and then eyes me mischievously. "You know who *I'm* shipping nowadays?" she asks.

"Who?" I ask distractedly.

"You and Alix."

I spit out my croissant at the exact moment everyone

appears at the patio door, and Trissa busts out laughing.

"You'll pay for that," I mutter.

"Pay for what?" Zora asks as she, Alix, and Shrey reach the yard.

"Nothing," I say, trying to destroy Trissa with my side-eye.

"Need any more snacks?" Dad calls. "Cereal, madam?" he says directly to Trissa.

"Can I live here?" she asks him.

"I think your parents would object," Dad says. "Why don't you join me in the kitchen again?"

Trissa follows behind him like a sugar-starved puppy dog.

"Hey," Shrey says once they've left. "Is it cool if I show Zora our *Avatar* collectibles? You still have them out, right?"

OBSERVATIONS:

- Shrey holds his gaze directly on Zora, as if he can't drag it away.
- Zora smiles slyly at Alix.

CONCLUSION: They are definitely leaving so that they can hold hands or kiss in my

room where no one can see them. I may have
to figure out some way to de-cootie-fy my
room.

I'm a hundred percent right, but I wave my hand in
tacit approval.

"So," Alix says when they leave, "thanks for inviting
us over." The messy bun bobbles atop her head as she
talks. It's a bit hypnotic.

"Of course," I say.

"Zora's been in a funk since the whole Sarina thing.
She keeps wondering if *she* did something wrong."

"No way," I say, shaking my head. "She's not the one
who stole or wrote ransom notes."

"That's what I keep telling her. I wish she'd get that
you can't control what people think of you. Sarina's going
to think what she wants, but Zora is the best friend a girl
could have."

Thinking of Ethan Navarez, I say, "It's really hard to
accept that you could be the villain in someone's story."

"Deep!" Alix says approvingly. "Hey, speaking of
villains, did you hear Kenzie might be leaving school?
Her dad is furious."

"At her or the school?" I ask.

"The school," Alix says, looking annoyed. "For

suspending her. Like, what? They're supposed to *not* punish her for stealing? Come on!"

"Maybe she'll go to that private school after all," I say wryly.

"At least everyone got their stuff back," Alix says. "I think I saw Liz Davis hugging her makeup yesterday. And Juan looked so happy wearing that watch again."

Laughing, I tell her, "Brian is equally excited about his Jordans. He keeps sending me shoe selfies."

"In all seriousness, though," Alix says, eyeing me. "You made that happen."

I blush. "And the rest of you," I point out. "I'm not going to lie—it helps to have a whole *gang* of crime-solvers on my side."

"Happy to be in your sidecar, so to speak," Alix says, looking at me long enough that I flush and look away.

Motioning to the empty chair next to me, I say, "Um, do you want to sit?"

"Actually, I've been dying to ask you something," she says, her eyes twinkling.

Oof. The acrobats are back in *full* force.

"Yeah?" I ask.

"Shrey told Zora, and Zora told *me* . . ." She trails off a bit and for a terrifying second I wonder if somehow she's figured out that I maybe-like her. I brace myself for impact, until she says the words I never expect to hear: ". . . that you guys made a *crime board* to find Kenzie and Sarina."

"Oh!" I say. "We did. Do you want to see?"

"Um, yes!"

I open the patio door and show her into the living room, where the crime board is still propped up from when Dad had been admiring it the night before.

"Whoa. Red yarn. Very old-school cool," she says, looking down at the board again. "This is, like . . . *intense.*"

I can practically feel my face fall. "That's me. Super intense and creepy."

She gives me a funny look, but not an unkind one. "Nobody said you were creepy."

"That's what everyone says," I say. "I'm 'that creepy girl who draws skulls all the time.'"

"I don't think that about you at all." Alix smiles at me a bit crookedly, holding my gaze, and I can feel myself blushing again. She looks like she has really soft skin.

Wait, *what*? I'm looking at her *skin*? I am creepy.

I'm Queen Creepy of Creeptopia.

"Hey," Alix says, reaching for the coffee table. "*In the Shadow of a Killer.* Signed? So cool."

I break out of my self-deprecating spiral about

noticing Alix's skin, and stare at her, mouth agape. "You know that book too?"

Alix laughs. "You think after listening to *Game Over* I wasn't going to look this one up? I mean, the Masterpiece Man was nasty, but this is *serial killer* territory. I couldn't put it down."

I open my mouth to ask her approximately one thousand questions, but Shrey and Zora walk into the living room at that moment. Trissa isn't far behind, trying not to spill a large bowl of cereal. On her way to the couch, she looks at the book in Alix's hands, then back up at me knowingly.

I give her a look that says, *Don't even start.*

Once we're all sitting on our large sectional, however, Trissa makes an excellent point. "You know, friends, technically we've all got money to burn. Each of us was willing to risk our portion of the hundred bucks, right?"

"That's not really money to burn," I say with a laugh. "It's only money we didn't use on a ransom. Besides, I'll have to use some of the twenty I got back to pay you for glitter supplies."

"I can put in for that too," Shrey says.

"And me!" Zora adds, while Alix raises her hand to join in.

"Nice! Maybe I can buy that new ink," I say, pumping

my fist victoriously.

"Okay, so maybe we don't really have extra money," Alix says. "But I have a question. What would you all buy if you had a hundred bucks and you *had* to spend it?" Alix asks.

Trissa looks thoughtful. "I can't put it toward my Lego Millennium Falcon fund?"

"No, you have to spend it!" Alix says.

Zora smiles. "Probably get another display case for my rocks. I've got some really cool geodes that need a shadow box."

Shrey swoons. "That is so cool. Hey, Zora, tell them the joke from the other day."

She looks embarrassed. "Um, okay. Why wouldn't the geologist give up his rocks?" She looks around at us, but we're all clearly stumped. "They had *sedimental* value."

It's pretty cheesy, but we all giggle nonetheless.

"What about you, Shrey? What would you buy?" Alix asks.

"I would preorder the new Paper Mario," Shrey declares. "And then four Taqueria Tlaquepaque burritos."

"Oh, *Origami King*?" Alix says. "Good one. Also, I approve of the burritos."

"Drew?" Alix asks. She gives me the same crooked grin *again*. "A whole sampler set of ink? A fresh corkboard and top-of-the-line yarn for your crime board? A first edition of *In the Shadow of a Killer*? All the *Crime and Waffles* merch you can handle?"

"Something like that," I say, smiling back.

But, at this moment, I'm not thinking about mysteries. I'm thinking that, for the first time I can remember, I'm looking at my house without picturing my mother walking out the door forever. And I'm thinking that I'm *not* scared of my dad or any of my friends leaving me behind. Not anymore.

Lita Miyamoto says that some people live with one person's voice in their head. Usually it's the worst voice—the one that tells you you're kidding yourself, or that you're not enough. Sometimes, she says, that's why people do bad things. They can't escape that one voice. Maybe that's why Sarina did what she did.

Sure, I have a mom who underestimates me sometimes. And maybe other people will down the road. But I also have a choice. I can listen to that mean voice. Or I can choose to ignore it. Because my future is exactly that—*mine*.

I may not know a lot about being a regular seventh-grade girl, but I know this: that choice makes me one of the lucky ones.

ACKNOWLEDGMENTS

My family will always be at the forefront here because, without their faith in me and relentless enthusiasm, I would never have had the courage to pursue publishing. Thanks to my wonderful and patient husband and soulmate, Ben, without whom none of this would be possible. My amazing daughter, Mia: you inspire me, and remain one of the best storytellers I've ever met. I love you, sweetheart, and one day the Master Bagel will be canon!

To my mother: thanks for being the polar opposite of Jennifer Leclair. You edited my first novel—written at the age of thirteen—and are the queen of the Murderinos. For Maren, my wonderful (ten years younger) twin sister, you are my forever first reader and you are legitimately *why* I write books. You are also the best webmaster and author personal trainer a girl could ask for.

Karim, you are my brother and my first line of defense. Please keep highlighting sentences and just saying "NO." You're nearly always right. Katie, you have been so positive about making sure my voice gets into the world and I am forever appreciative. I love you both so dearly. Thanks to my wonderful Grandma June, who taught me not to put off dreams because life gets in the way. Also, a hat tip to my fantastic friends—you know who you are, and you're all family to me.

Chelsea Eberly, what can I say? You're an absolute *rock star* of an agent. You know my books better than I do. I'm so honored and grateful to have worked with you these past few years and I look forward to years more! Much appreciation also to the whole Greenhouse team, and to The Rights People for helping bring this character worldwide.

Emilia Rhodes, you believed in this book from day one. Aside from being an amazing editor, you always take the time to give me insight, answer my questions, and help me take this character to the next level. Molto grazie to the whole Clarion and HarperCollins team, especially Elizabeth Agyemang, Sammy Brown, Emily Mannon, Laura Mock, Melissa Cicchitelli, and Heather Tamarkin. Also, I need to shout from the rooftops about Alba Filella. Alba, you somehow climbed into my head and saw *exactly* what these characters looked like for the cover art. I'm blown away by your work.

Without readers, where would I be? Eva, you are my CP and my absolute rock. I'm grateful every day for what we've built together. Thanks to Naakai Addy and Audris Candra for your thoughtful insights into Drew's journey this time around. I'm so appreciative of my fabulous '22 Debuts for reading, as well as my middle grade critique group, and all the kids who picked up the first book and loved it.

I want to say a sincere thanks to a few groups that really helped me get through this draft. First, librarians. To me, you are the ultimate guardians and protectors of our books, and I am forever appreciative of the work you do to fight censorship. A shout out as well to "That's Messed Up: An SVU Podcast," which helped me stay in true crime mode while drafting. And, as always, thanks to Michelle McNamara—one of the main inspirations as I wrote this character, and whom I see as a real-life Lita Miyamoto.

Finally, to my number one fan, my father: your love and your support stay with me even though you're gone. I love you, Dad.